Rowan

Celest G. Boyle

Contents

Chapter One

C hapter One:

I knew one day my talent would be the reason I met Death in person, whether it be willingly or by force. I just didn't know when that would be or what shape it would take form in.

"Come here, my darling," I said softly while sitting down, the grass beneath acting as a pillow.

I watched him sniff the air, awaiting whatever trap I may have. We remained like that for several minutes until he took a hesitant step forward, his hooves silent against the ground.

"It's okay," I promised, slowly putting out my hand with my palm up and opened, revealing the crisp, green slices of apple I had for him.

His tawny ears flickered at the sight of the unusual food and his black nose twitched. I had fed him several times before, but he still wasn't ready to trust me. I supposed I wouldn't trust a human either, after the horrid things we had done to his kind.

It took time, but it was worth it when the slender fawn finally came to me. He stretched out his long neck so he wouldn't have to come too close and took the food from my palm. I smiled, laughing quietly when he licked up the small bits left.

"See, not all of us are bad," I told him, receiving a head-tilt in return.

I reached out as slowly as possible, seeing his muscles coil at the movement. Still, he hadn't left yet.

"My Todd would be jealous if he knew I was giving another animal affection," I told the fawn and continued to talk when my hand grazed him.

He jumped at the contact but with soothing words, he calmed down. He started closer to me, but his ears flickered again and just like that, he was gone.

I sighed and stood, brushing the dirt and grass off my dress. I was sure he had heard something that I would soon hear too.

I was proven right when I became aware of the sound of a distant voice, echoing in the quiet area: "She's done nothing wrong! You have no need for her!"

I paused, my heart quickening. I knew the voice—that frantic sound would be familiar anywhere. I traveled through the dense forest, walking fast, everything else forgotten.

What I found wasn't what I had expected. There was my father, surrounded by large horses as black as night. They were huge in comparison to the animals I was used to, yet far more gentle.

On top of them were men, covered in thick armor from head to toe; the only part visible were their expressionless eyes. I could see weapons strapped around their waists and I panicked, knowing my father was defenseless.

"What's going on, Papa?" I asked, walking towards the older man who was trying his best to hold himself together.

At the sound of my voice, the men turned together, all eyes on me. It was frightening that they had done so in unison, not a single one off-beat. I resisted the urge to shiver at the intensity of their weighted gazes.

I made my way to the middle, standing close by my father who put a shaking arm around me. His eyes were wide and round with fear, his limbs quivering. Never had I seen him so afraid.

"Are you Rowan?"

The voice responsible for the question was deep and commanding, as if saying no wasn't an option. My eyes met his, refusing to let him intimidate me. I had seen far worse than him—scaring me wouldn't be easy.

"What business do you have here? My father and I have done nothing wrong," I said with an edge to my voice. We were the only ones who lived in the forest, as we preferred.

The man nodded to his men and did nothing else. The simple movement caused them to jump from their horses and swarm on us, yanking me from my father. I screamed for him and fought as hard as I could, but it was useless when their grips were like clamps of steel.

They dragged him away, towards the general direction of our house. If they hurt him in the slightest way, I would ensure they knew just what the wildlife here was capable of.

"Calm down; we mean no harm. Your father is being taken back to your home, and I will assist you there after we have talked."

My head whipped in the direction of the voice and I yanked myself away from the men holding me. They let go after a moment, allowing me to put some distance between us. I considered running towards my father, but I knew I wouldn't make it far before they grabbed me once again.

"What do you want?" I asked shortly, crossing my arms, praying that the men truly wouldn't cause harm to my father.

He looked at me for a moment before taking off his helmet, revealing a head of blonde, almost white, hair. His mouth was set in a straight line, as emotionless as his eyes.

"We are in need of your assistance. You can help us willingly, or we can force you to help," he commanded and I laughed harshly. Threats were meaningless in the forest where the animals roamed. Here, I was the one in control.

"What can I offer you? I'm not familiar with anything but the forest and its life. I don't think I will be of much help," I explained, but deep down I knew it was futile. I knew why he was here and what he wanted from me. No one ever came through this forest, and certainly not guards.

His eyes flickered before he responded, "Are you not Rowan, Tamer of Animals? Are you not the one whispered about throughout the lands, the one people fear?"

I pursed my lips, looking at the trees around us. They were tall: their thick roots hugged the ground as they stretched towards the sky; their leaves snatched up the sun's rays. They had so much beauty, yet it seemed no one else saw it.

"If you were smart, you would fear me too," I finally replied, my eyes landing on the man.

From the corner of my eyes, I could see the others looking at one another, wondering if they had made a mistake. But the man didn't even flinch at my words.

"I'll tell you the details of what you are doing when we are closer to the castle. We have a long way to travel," he said, ignoring my words. Had he simply not heard me, or had something far worse been thrown at him during his lifetime?

"If I help, how do I know my father will be okay? I'm the only one here to take care of him," I said, but it seemed he'd expected me to ask that.

"There is a town nearby. We'll place him there when we're assured you won't run. Then, you're free to visit him as you please."

The town was surely better than him living in the forest alone. The one nearest to us wouldn't welcome him because of me, but another town? They may have heard rumors, but they weren't likely to know anything about my father.

"He is to be given a servant when placed into the town. I don't want him working when his back doesn't allow him to. He's also to be given a nice home, not something you'd stuff your peasants in. I want him treated kindly, as he deserves," I said, meeting his stare head-on.

I knew I shouldn't be making demands, certainly not when I was outnumbered. But I knew I wouldn't be able to do anything when I was worrying about my father. If my father was fine and living well, I would be able to focus.

The man began circling me, walking slowly. I could hear his boots scraping against the ground as if it had wronged him in some way. He was assessing me, challenging me to look at him. But I held my head up higher, ignoring the urge to turn towards him.

"I need confirmation that you are Rowan. Once that is given, I can agree to your conditions. You will also be given money for your assistance, a large amount."

My eyes flickered at the end of his sentence. I loved living in the forest more than anything. Here, I was able to use my talent freely. The animals had grown used to me; some even walking up to me during the day. Here, I was free of human judgement for my difference.

However, living in the forest was hard on my father. He was getting older, and his back was getting worse. Ever since he'd messed it up, he wasn't allowed to work by himself—although he still tried. It was hard for him to move around and drive into town when we needed essential items. Living in a town away from here would be so much easier on him.

I took a deep breath before answering: "I am Rowan, Tamer of Animals. I'm the one who can tame the wildest of beasts. I'm the one who can turn the most loyal dog against its owner. I am the one people fear."

Chapter Two

‐‐

This one is dedicated to the rude-ass helping me edit <3

Chapter Two:

"You can't be serious."

"You cannot expect me to follow you into a mysterious land alone. I will bring him, and that's final."

He stared at me with a piercing look, as if he would give anything to strangle me on the spot. I supposed he would've preferred a gentle, obedient girl. It was a shame that he was stuck with me.

"That thing is barely alive. Leave him here with your father and he'll be allowed in the town," he tried but I shook my head.

"He may be missing a leg and his tail, but my little one is better off than you are. And he isn't fond of anyone but me, not even my father," I explained, holding the bright orange ball of fur closer to my chest.

"You aren't worth this much trouble," he muttered, running a hand through his hair with an irritated look. Good, I was finally getting to him. Maybe he would get the sense that I didn't want to go anywhere with him.

"Bring him," he decided before directing his men to take my two suitcases and tie them up.

I smiled down at the reynard in my arms, pressing my lips against his soft fur. Todd had been the first animal I'd tamed. We were both younger at the time when Todd was mauled by something much larger than himself. I had only wanted to help him, not yet realizing what I was able to do.

"Rowan!"

I turned and met my father who enveloped me into his arms, a grouchy fox smothered between us. We said our parting words, and I quickly kissed him goodbye before the tears rebelled against me. I wouldn't cry in front of these strangers.

"You'll ride with me and I'll explain the situation."

I watched as the man put his helmet back on before meeting my gaze. The only thing I could see were his light brown eyes, waiting on my response. I walked over, not allowing him to intimidate me as I carefully placed Todd into a bag. I gently slung it over my shoulder, hearing his soft chatter in my ears.

"You now know my name, but I have nothing to call you by. That does not seem the least bit fair," I told the stranger as I walked over to his horse.

She was beautiful for such a large animal, yet I could see the gentle nature she held within her deep eyes. They were as dark as the hair that covered her, shining with eagerness to obey. She looked at me, her muscles coiled, ready to spring.

"Perhaps you should give me a name so that I can remember you by something?" I said, smiling at the horse. I murmured words of affection to her, reaching up to stroke her muzzle.

She leaned into my hand, warm air blowing out her flared nostrils. "Such a beautiful creature," I whispered, placing my forehead against hers. I closed my eyes, feeling her relax under my hand as I stroked her neck.

"You can call me Sage," he said, finally responding to me.

I opened my eyes, feeling Sage's own on me as I stroked the horse. I stiffened when I realized the others were watching me too, captivated. I wasn't used to anyone around me when I was with animals. It seemed like something that was private, something others didn't deserve to see.

I pulled away from her, saying goodbye before walking over to him again. "You're lucky to have such a magnificent animal," I said, and he simply looked at me before ordering his men onto their own horses.

Sage climbed onto his in a fluid motion before offering me his hand. I huffed at him but grabbed it, swinging onto the back of the horse. I rubbed her, thanking her for allowing me to ride her when Sage cleared his throat.

"What?" I asked, already irritated by him. He was a human, someone who didn't deserve the respect animals did-forcing me to go with him only proved my point.

"You'll need to hold onto me. It will be easier for the both of us," he explained and I frowned, wishing for a horse of my own.

I leaned closer to him, wrapping my arms around his waist. Underneath his armor, I could feel his chest expanding with his breath. I had never been so close to anyone in my life, and it terrified me.

"Let us leave," I muttered, already missing the forest. I couldn't bear the thought of leaving it for a foreign land.

I made it a silent promise that I would return one day. I would return to its trees and grass, to its fawns and wolves. I would return to the only place that was truly a home for me.

Sage barked an order, one that sent the other horses flying, their powerful hooves beating against the ground at an irregular tempo. Not a second later, we were flying too, heading to take the lead in front of the others.

I made the mistake of glancing back. There stood my father, waving at me, tears washing his face. However, he wasn't alone. In the shadows of the trees were several animals, all standing there. They were watching at me, every one of them familiar with my touch.

When I could no longer see them, I heard the sound of a howl, long and sorrowful. Other wolves joined in, and it was only then that I allowed my tears to run free.

Chapter Three

The ride was uneventful. There was complete silence except for when the wind became playful, rustling our clothes and the trees' leaves. Sage hadn't said a single word, not yet explaining what he desired from me.

The sun had become tired long ago and settled down for the night, allowing the moon a turn to shine. The moon was our guidance, giving us light in the darkness.

"We will set camp out here for the night," Sage commanded, his voice shattering the silence.

The men pulled their horses to a stop before sliding off and tying them up. I dropped from Sage's horse without his help before letting Todd out of the bag.

He zipped off, surely to inspect the place. I wasn't worried because I knew he would be back within a few minutes. Todd never ventured far without me and knew better than to stray.

We were in the middle of a large clearing surrounded by red oak trees and little patches of bushes here and there. There was no wildlife to be seen, all hiding from the predators: humans.

Sage slipped off his horse and tied her up, stroking her muzzle. I watched curiously, noting that she seemed elated to have his attention. He was murmuring to her, a light smile on his face as he did so.

Sage adored his horse, more so than anyone I had met. It was odd, seeing a man have so much affection for an animal who was more than happy to return it. His horse pressed her head against his, closing her eyes when he rubbed her ears.

"Odd, isn't it, Todd?" I asked softly when I felt fur being pressed against my leg. I didn't have to look down to know it was my little one rubbing against me.

Sage spotted me and patted his horse one last time before he began walking over. When he was within reach, he began talking.

"We're going to spend the night here. We'll eat in the morning and then set off. Another two days of this and we should be there.

For the night, you will be sharing a tent with me," he explained and I gave him a look.

"I would rather spend the night lying on the grass than sleeping with a stranger," I told him, and he frowned in return.

"I would rather you did too. But I cannot risk you escaping on me or the King hearing that I treated you poorly," he said and I tensed. The King?

"Are you going to tell me what I'm doing, or are you going to continue to leave me in the dark?" I asked, brazen accusation in my words. He needed to tell me sooner than later.

"Yes, after I've helped my men set up camp," he replied and proceeded to leave me, joining the others.

It didn't take them long to set up the dark tents and place a large pile of wood in the middle. It became clear to me that they were used to this and worked together efficiently.

"This is our tent," Sage said, holding up the black flap for me, a lantern in his other hand. I hesitated before stepping in.

There were covers on the bottom for cushioning, but other than that, it was empty. I found myself sitting next to the edge of the tent, realizing how little room there was.

Todd had been right on my heels and was now sniffing the tent, darting around it. When Sage came in he bared his teeth, his ears flattening against his head.

The only source of lighting was the one the lantern provided, which was dim. I could see the outline of Sage but not much else.

"It's alright, my little one," I coaxed, beckoning Todd over with a finger. He was more than happy to crawl into my lap but kept his eyes on Sage.

"How does it work? Can you not truly tame animals?" He asked, pointing to Todd who was still baring his teeth.

"Animals are similar to us, only superior in nature. It takes them a while to get used to people, just as we take some time getting used to strangers. Todd would be equivalent to an introvert," I explained, running my nails along Todd's back.

He momentarily forgot about Sage and focused on me once again, chattering. "Then you cannot tame the animals for others? They are only tame for you?" Sage asked.

"It's not just for me; it's around me. Wait," I told him and pulled Todd close, whispering in his ear and supplying him with an abundance of affection.

"Do you have food?" I asked him and his eyes flickered before he pulled a piece of slim, dried meat from his pocket.

"Hold it out in your palm, face up," I instructed, the movement catching Todd's attention.

Todd crept over to Sage, his body hunched together. I watched as Todd inspected the meat before snatching it up. After devouring it, he climbed over Sage, searching for more.

After seeing Sage's startled expression, I laughed. "I didn't do anything to Todd; my talent is more natural than that. Todd is willing to love anyone who offers him food."

Todd's nose was now planted at Sage's pocket, nudging it forcefully where I assumed the rest of the meat was. He started chattering excitedly at Sage, who was trying to pull back his smile.

"Todd, my dear, leave him alone," I said, and he crawled over to me once again, disappointment in his eyes. Todd loved food and the person who fed it to him more than anything.

"If you don't know how my talent works, then why am I here?" I asked Sage, both of us sobering up at the question.

"Because you're our only hope," he said quietly, his words as grim as his expression.

I couldn't imagine what I was hope for if it was enough to worry him and the other men, so I asked: "And just what am I the hope for?"

He was looking at the entrance of the tent as if he were elsewhere. He was quiet for a moment before saying, "Have you heard of King Sandalius?"

My body tensed at the name, the air chilling around us. Todd noticed my sudden mood change and began growling. Or possibly, he too knew what danger the name held.

"Everyone has," I responded, not sure what to say. If this involved King Sandalius, there would be no kindness where I was going.

"And you've heard about his . . . primal side?" He asked, his eyes flickering to me.

"You mean the fact he's half-animal?" I clarified as if it wasn't a big deal.

Everyone had heard of King Sandalius and his legendary story. He was abandoned as a child by his parents who left him in a basket in the middle of a forest.

He had cried and cried, but his parents weren't the ones who'd answered him. The wolves showed him compassion and took care of him instead. They had been his family, the ones who'd fought for and protected him.

He'd grown up with them within the forest until a group of hunters found him. By that time, he was a strong, teen boy. The wolves fought to keep him-he was one of theirs-but in the end, they were all slaughtered.

The boy was taken in, and the King and his wife took a liking to him. They adored the boy and welcomed him into their home, as they couldn't have children of their own. They helped him learn the ways of their society and taught him about the love of humans.

However, Prince Sandalius quickly became very well-known. When two people came to the castle demanding that he was their son, they were turned away and denied access despite their pleading.

They were desperate to get their son back for unknown reasons, maybe because of the guilt that clawed at them every night. So they went to seek the help of an infamous witch who promised to give the boy back to his parents.

The witch went into the castle as a guest and when she was close enough to Prince Sandalius, she revealed herself. She then told the boy she would give him back to his parents, the ones who raised him.

She changed him into a wolf and said his parents were the wolves, the only ones who had ever treated him as their child. She said it would teach humans that animals weren't the problem: they were. Prince Sandalius would remain human, but when his primal side took over, he would become the very creature that raised him.

What the witch didn't expect was for the Prince to handle it poorly. His primal side began taking over more often than not, and in a rage, he killed the King. Humans became more fearful of the wolves than ever and began hunting them with a passion. They tried to kill Prince Sandalius as well, although it failed miserably.

Now, he was King and ruled over thousands of acres of land. He did so well, but only because he was feared by all. Guests hadn't been allowed near the castle in years, and from what I had heard, servants were recently running away too.

"Yes, he is half-animal. And you're expected to tame that half."

Chapter Four

I had thought better of Sage, but apparently I was wrong. He wasn't fearless. He was simply crazy.

"I tame animals, if that! I don't tame humans!" I snapped at him, my disbelief clouding my fear.

"He's half-animal. It is that side that needs your magic touch, not the human side. You tame animals, and this is no different," Sage explained right before he had the audacity to blow out the lantern.

I waited, thinking perhaps this was a joke. But I heard him stir as he lay down for the night, and I realized he was completely serious. He wanted me to tame the King, the only true beast in this world.

I flew out the tent, welcoming the cool air against my heated skin. It was a mere blessing in comparison to Sage's request.

I continued walking in no particular direction. I just needed to get away from them, away from what they wanted. Getting lost in the forest would be a joy for me at this moment.

So that was exactly what I did, my descending mood lifting. I was far enough away that I couldn't see the camp setup or hear any of its sounds. I could sense the animals nearby, wondering if they needed to scurry farther.

I slid down the firm trunk of a tree, resting my back against it. I needed to think about this, especially if I wanted to leave the castle alive.

They wanted me to tame the King, something I knew I couldn't do. When I was around others, particularly humans, my harsh personality tended to reveal itself. They were cold and relentless to the animals, so I acted the same to them.

It had become a habit, one that hasn't yet caused me any trouble. People stopped attempting to talk and would travel down a longer path if it meant avoiding me. Fortunately, I was happy with that because I wanted nothing to do with them either.

However, that habit was now going to contribute to my ultimate death. The King was known for his very short temper and, equally, a short patience for others. He would grow frustrated with my ways and decide it would benefit him to kill me.

I knew running right now wouldn't get me very far. They would find me with ease and drag me back. It would only give them reason to watch me more carefully. They also knew where I lived and would make it faster to my father on horse than I would on foot.

So were running or dying my only two options? They couldn't be; there had to be one option that didn't end badly. I just wasn't sure what it was at the moment—but I would find it.

A tree nearby rustled and I glanced up, seeing Sage with an orange ball right at his heels. Todd came to me first and I pulled him against me, hugging him. It wasn't much, but his presence was a comfort.

Sage knelt beside me and out of the corner of my eye, I could see him looking at the ground, considering his words before he began speaking to me.

"I know the horrible stories you've heard about King Sandalius. I understand why you are scared; it's reasonable," he started before glancing over at me.

"He may have done those things, but that's not all he is. He's composed of more than his destructive actions, and most don't look past that.

You, however, can. You see past human intellect and see the cruelty upon which we pride ourselves. You see what others cannot, Rowan. I need you to do that now, for the safety of others."

I laughed softly. "The safety of others? Do you think I care about humans? If they died off, perhaps the animals would have a chance at peace," I replied, spotting his frown. He didn't agree with my opinions, like everyone else.

People thought I was being hypocritical when I voiced myself. I wanted others to die, but was I willing to die? The answer had always been yes to me, as I would sacrifice myself if it was worth doing.

"You don't understand. King Sandalius agrees with you. He would rather see the humans killed off than lose nature and its wildlife. He hates them for slaughtering his true family," he tried, but only sighed when he didn't receive a response.

"I will make you a deal. If you can tame the King, I'll convince him to declare an end to hunting within the forest you live in. No one will be allowed to kill or harm the animals there, whether for sport or food."

I turned with surprise at his words before I narrowed my eyes. There was a loophole somewhere; there had to be. Why else would he offer to help me in such a large way?

As if he could read my mind, he replied, "I know I have no reason to help you, but King Sandalius has saved my life more times than I can count. I'm willing to do whatever I can to help him in the same way before he drives himself off the edge of a cliff."

The longer I looked at Sage, the more I realized he truly cared for the King. The King was someone who meant a lot to him and was probably very close. He was willing to help this human, or beast, with the same determination I used to help the animals.

"Will this be placed in writing when we arrive?" I asked him, needing something to solidify the deal.

"Yes, if that's what you prefer," he replied, his voice lighter than before.

I nodded, standing up with Todd still bundled in my arms. Todd was content, his eyes drifting shut despite being held like an infant. He was my baby, my little one, in every sense.

"Then all is okay?" Sage asked as also he stood up while I smoothed down my dress.

"No, all is not okay. I'm not okay with you taking me to a place where death resides, but I'm willing to make the sacrifice if it means you will keep your promise," I replied, and Sage gave me a look conveying he wasn't pleased with my answer.

Did he want me to smile and beg him to tell me all about the King? Did he want me to sing and skip during our travels? I wasn't thrilled with what was happening and certainly didn't want to take part in it.

"We should go back," Sage replied and led the way.

We returned to the quiet campsite, where snoring had begun. Todd jumped out of my arms and into the forest to explore once again.

I crawled into the tent with Sage following behind. I was first to lie down, my back turned to him, but I could still hear the covers beneath us rustle as he lay down as well. If I paid closer attention, I would have noticed our body heat mixing with one another between us, making him seem that much closer.

It took a while, but I could hear his breathing slow down into even, almost silent breaths. I almost thought perhaps I would never join him.

But sleep surprised me by taking me soon after.

*side-note: would y'all be interested in me sending out holiday cards?

Chapter Five

So here's how this will work. For the next month, I will be updating on a schedule! This is being done so that I'll have a full month to dedicate just to the Property of a Gordon Rewrite. Once this month is up, I'll return to my poor updating haha. Come back every Friday for an update!

The mornings were brutal in comparison to the rest of the day. I was woken up by yelling each time: Sage telling his men that it was time to get ready. I was never able to go back to sleep, as the noise didn't stop until nighttime.

They would all multitask. Some would cook a small breakfast for us while others worked on putting everything up. Then there would be those who fed the horses and put the equipment on them.

The rides through the forest were dull, for the most part. The horse marched together through the thickets of foliage, with Sage occasionally barking orders at the others.

Once, we passed a deer. The guards said they could hunt it down and kill it for meat but I objected. I told them they were free to kill for food on their own time, but I wouldn't allow them to do so while I was there. Fortunately, by the time we all stopped arguing about the issue, the deer was long gone.

The nights were equal parts of silence and noise. They would talk when they finished setting up the equipment; some would even sing with bellowing voices. The noise would gradually descend as they began announcing their departure for the night, one by one. Silence would then take the place of noise until the sun rose, beginning the cycle once again.

"There are a few things you should be aware of before meeting the King today."

I turned towards Sage, opening my backpack as I did so. Todd walked over and hopped in without having to be told. I swung it over my shoulder before finally giving Sage my full attention.

"Are you going to tell me or wait until I guess correctly?" I asked, my voice dripping with sarcasm. This trip had stripped away any of my sympathy for the King and his guards.

They had taken me from my home and from my forest. It would be a long time before I finally saw my father or the forest's animals again, all because of them.

Sage narrowed his eyes, finally giving a sign that my temper was affecting him. "If you talk to the King like that, you will not last long. That is certain."

"I've heard about his horrid temper. It seems as if I breathe wrong, I will be harmed. So does my attitude truly make a difference?" I snapped back and he clenched his jaw.

"He is as human as you and I, Rowan. He just needs help to see that," he said, taking a deep breath before looking up at the sky as if the world's solutions were written there.

I hesitated before walking closer to him, the grass beneath me stirring. "Perhaps the King only needs a friend, not to be tamed. Perhaps, all he needs is someone to place his trust in," I tried, and Sage's eyes hardened within seconds as he glanced back at me.

"Do you think I haven't tried helping him and that I stand by as he gets worse? I would not have come to you if it did anything," he replied coldly and harshly, enough so that I took a step back in surprise.

Sage caught the action but turned his attention towards his men. "If we want to be there before night, we need to leave now!" He snapped, and that was it. He no longer felt the need to warn me about the King's tendencies or even talk to me.

The men got on their horses and I watched Sage climb onto his, running a hand through her mane. It was amazing how soft he could be with her when he acted so harshly with me.

I climbed on after Sage, feeling his body coil when my arms wrapped around him. "If I had a choice, I wouldn't be touching you," I remarked, his body tensing further.

"And if I had a choice, you wouldn't be talking," he muttered back before commanding his men to move.

The ride was characteristically quiet, but the tension curled itself between Sage and I spoke volumes. It teemed, waiting to snatch one of us up and make a scene.

I ignored it as best as I could, focusing on the forest surrounding us. We were a few hours through the journey when the forest ended, presenting a long, dusty dirt road.

The horses turned, trotting along the path. I could tell by the sudden murmuring among the guards that we were close to our destination.

We veered left, the dirt path our guidance. The more the guards talked, the faster my heart started beating. It knew we could very well be heading to the place where it would stop permanently.

Even Todd was becoming restless, sensing something was off. He squirmed in my backpack, chattering softly in my ear.

I shushed him, but all it did was stop his movement. He continued to chatter away at me as if he was waiting for a true response, but I couldn't give him one.

Abruptly, the men started pointing forward, some grinning and laughing. I held my head up to see past Sage's shoulder and try to catch a glimpse of what they were so thrilled about—at the sight alone, my breath caught in my throat.

Peering above the trees in front of us was a large building, larger than any I had ever seen. It stood proudly tall, its top half transforming into either pointed, scaly roofs or thick, hindering towers. I was already in awe and I had yet to see the lower half.

What caught my attention most were the gargoyle-like statues that stood on top of various points of the castle. They were large enough that I could make out the shape of several wolves, even from this far away. The wolves were portrayed as gruesome, their teeth bared to display the canines everyone was afraid of.

I frowned, my sympathy for the King disappearing. He was part of the reason wolves had been hunted to near extinction. When a wolf ventured into a town, people would claim it thirsted for blood when it had been merely curious. It was then they decided wolves needed to be hunted down before they killed any humans.

I had personally been near wolves within the forest, and they weren't monsters or savages. That was a title I reserved solely for humans, who selfishly considered only one side of the story. The wolves were majestic and inquisitive, nothing like the displays King Sandalius had set up.

The castle grew in size as we went through the woods in front of us, taking a shortcut. I instinctively pressed closer to Sage, my nerves taking over. I was grateful he remained silent.

Then just like that, the wooded area ended and all that stood in front of us was the castle, home of King Sandalius—the man who I would tame or be killed by.

Chapter Six

"Command someone to make sure Rowan's room is prepared. If it is not, make sure they do so."

"Inform King Sandalius of our arrival. However, make sure he isn't busy."

Even here, where there were much more people scurrying around, it was clear Sage was still in charge. It was him who directed everyone around, telling the servants to put the horses back in the stable, to take my things to my room.

"That won't be necessary," he said quickly when someone reached for the reins of his horse. "I'll take Sequeria myself."

"Such a beautiful name," I murmured, catching his attention. He grabbed her reins, talking to her softly before he began pulling her in my direction. She obeyed him, nickering quietly.

"You will go with me. We will see the King together, as he instructed that I be with you every time the two of you meet," Sage explained, leading Sequeria to the stables. I followed, deciding it was better than waiting here until he returned.

We walked around the castle, towards the edge of the forest to the gray stable. It was beautiful, not as faded or weathered down as I imagined it would be. It was also large, housing more horses than I could count.

We walked into the dimly lit stable, and the smell of fresh hay and horse manure surrounded us. The horses were silent: their heavy breathing was all I could hear, along with the occasional hoof-stomp.

Sage found his way to the end where the very last stall was tucked into the far corner of the stable. He opened it and gently took everything off Sequeria, talking to her as he did so. I found myself unable to resist a smile at the sight.

"I need to brush her down, and then we can leave," Sage said, and I took the time to take Todd out of my bag, placing him on the stable's floor. The moment his paws touched the ground, he darted away, out of the stable and my sight.

"You have a gentle way with her that most don't use with animals," I murmured when he was finally finished and began locking her stall.

"She and I have a bond that most don't create with them," he replied, stroking her one last time when she nudged him with her head.

Someone entered the stables and I turned, seeing an umber-skinned girl making her way towards us. When Sage finally turned, she grabbed her skirt and curtsied, bowing her head at the same time.

"Sir Coventry, King Sandalius awaits you and the guest," she said, her eyes never quite meeting his. Even that was a product of an animalistic hierarchy, and they didn't even seem to realize it.

"Yes, thank you, Shaterria. You're free to leave," he replied, and I could see her face darken at his words before she bowed once again and was off.

"First name basis with a peasant girl?" I asked, studying him. He didn't turn or even acknowledge my words. I thought perhaps he would ignore me.

"She is much more than a peasant among these lands. While I am the most trusted guard of King Sandalius, she is the most trusted worker. It is why she is sent to deliver his messages. She and I are the only ones allowed near him." His eyes flickered towards me as he added, "I suppose you are also an exception now."

"Is there anything I should know when approaching him?" I asked. I wanted to be as prepared as I could and avoid scheduling an early meeting with Death.

"Do not mention his past. It is a dark subject for him, one that is quick to set him off. He's been through more than he should have, and it's best not to bring any of it up. He does not need to relive it because of someone's mere curiosity," he said simply, making me wonder how often people were curious enough to ask about it.

"Do not challenge him in any way," he also added, shooting me a look that caused me to frown and cross my arms.

"What makes you think I would be stupid enough to challenge him?" I snapped back, watching as he shook his head.

"Crossed arms are a sign of defiance, as are meeting someone's gaze head-on. You won't even last a day if you continue as you have been. Talking back is also a sign of someone attempting to assert their dominance," he explained before looking over at me and waiting.

I almost did nothing, but with much reluctance and the sound of my teeth grinding against one another, I uncrossed my arms and let them fall to my side. He gave me another pointed look and I shot him a piercing one back before letting my gaze fall away from him.

He laughed softly, finding this amusing. When he noticed I hadn't joined in, he sighed and said, "Rowan, he has the same tendencies as the animals you lived with in your forest. Do you not have to submit to them in order to gain their trust?"

"The opposite actually," I replied quickly, jumping at the chance to prove him wrong. "You have to be firm with them. You have to be the Alpha among them, or they will take the chance to attack when they can.

If you submit to a dominant wolf, how far do you think you will get before they realize you are not of use to them? Every pack, skulk, and herd has some sort of system within its group. If you are not useful within the group, you are banished or killed."

He frowned at me, clearly not pleased with the direction this conversation had taken. "Please promise me you will not do the same with King Sandalius. If you attempt to challenge him, it will not end well. Do you understand? You are our last chance."

I didn't respond with the witty remark I had conjured up. Instead, I found myself noticing the desperation within his voice, the hope that was stitched onto its frayed edges. If I did not help, the kingdom would likely collapse as a result, putting a complete end to its journey. He could potentially lose everything.

"I promise," I said softly, watching his shoulders drop just the slightest at my words.

"Thank you," he said before he began walking out of the stable. I hesitated before following behind, wishing that perhaps someone would change their mind and I would no longer be needed here.

Sage opened his mouth to say something, but he turned slightly at the same time and the words were lost. I watched as his gaze traveled down me, causing me to stiffen, my arms crossing themselves again automatically.

"I cannot present you to the King," he muttered before catching the attention of another guard, who ran to where we were.

"Inform King Sandalius that Rowan and I will meet with him in an hour.
She has been traveling for several days, wearing the same dress, and is not
able to present herself to His Highness currently," he explained, causing
me to look down at my dress.

The ends looked as if they had seen better days, and the once white dress
now held patches of discolored brown from the dirt. Sage may have been
right, this once.

"Can the King not stand the sight of a little dirt?" I asked, knowing what
would happen.

Just as I predicted, Sage shot me a withering look and didn't bother responding. I suppose he was done talking to me and had gone back to saying
as little as possible. I smirked at his turned back, satisfied with the result.

Sage and I left the forested area, following the bricked road that led to the
castle, which seemed larger than I had originally thought. It could easily
house a hundred people and still have room for comfort.

Once the two guards saw Sage nearing, they were quick to grab and pull the
handles, the doors yawning open. They each gave Sage a silent nod when
we passed them, one Sage briefly returned.

I could feel the air leave my body before I heard someone gasp. I glanced up
at the ceiling that spiraled towards the sky, wondering if anyone ever had
the pleasure of touching it. There were intricate paintings up there, each
more beautiful than the first.

There were columns at the entrance of the place, proudly standing tall and
holding the structure up. The windows, much taller than I was, were being

cleaned at the very moment. The more I paid attention, the more I realized that there were people everywhere.

There were guards standing around, watching and seeing everything. There were servants scampering around like barn mice, finding something to keep them busy. This place was a world of its own—it was never still.

"Rowan."

I blinked, noticing Sage was watching me curiously. I hadn't moved from my spot, still taking everything in. I walked forward and he was off again.

I knew the forest and its wildlife back home better than anyone, yet when Sage turned the first corner, I was already lost. It seemed like an endless maze that held no exit.

A few minutes later, Sage finally slowed to a stop, opening the door that we stood in front of. "You will change in here. You can shower, if you would like, and by the time you finish, there will be clothing set on the edge of the bed. However, you need to be finished and presentable within less than an hour," he explained.

I nodded, at a loss for my sarcasm before stepping into the room.

Chapter Seven

The shower soothed my nerves, but the moment I stepped out and went into the room to search for the clothing, they began taking their crazed path once again.

There was a dress lying neatly on the bed's edge, appearing elegant in the room. I ran my fingers over the fabric, noting how soft it felt in comparison to the dresses I owned.

There was a pair of sandals at the foot of the bed. They had golden straps while the sandals were white, just like the dress.

I sighed and picked up the dress, surprised by how heavy the garment was. I questioned it once again, wondering just how much money had been placed and seamed into its fabric.

"Rowan, we need to leave soon," Sage called from the other side of the door, his voice expressionless. I glanced at the door in annoyance but didn't bother with a response. I would continue getting ready at this pace whether or not it pleased Sage.

I slid into the undergarments and the dress, both soft against my skin. They fit me perfectly, snug against my body. The white skirt spiraled down and grazed the floor; there was a slit along one side that boldly ended just above my thigh. The golden cord around my waist yearned for attention, bringing color to the dress. It was beautiful, much more so than anything I had ever worn.

I slipped into the sandals, adjusting the straps before taking a few deeps breaths. In just a few minutes, I would be standing in front of the King, someone who was well-known for his fatal temper. If I couldn't keep my own in check, I would perhaps be in serious trouble.

"Rowan," Sage started again and I huffed, swinging the door open before he could finish.

Sage's helmet was off and out of sight, allowing me to see his entire face. He too had cleaned up, based on the lack of dirt on his uniform. His eyes flickered, his mouth closing shut. I felt my body coil as his eyes traveled down, taking in the dress. His eyes finally found their way back to my own where he was met with a steely gaze.

"We should leave," he murmured, but before he could turn from me, I caught the reddening of his cheeks.

As Sage began walking, with me following closely behind, I noticed there were other guards trailing behind. I bit my lip to keep from snapping at them or rudely asking Sage why they were with us. It would only ruin my mood further, which wasn't wise before a meeting with the King.

We had been climbing stairs, but when we reached the top, Sage nodded to the other guards. I looked behind and watched as they nodded back before walking down the stairs, none of them staying.

"The King does not allow anyone within this part of the castle but Shaterria and I," he explained before pausing and added: "Along with yourself now."

I decided not to debate whether that was a good or a bad thing. I didn't think making a decision now would be best. However, a small part of me couldn't help but wonder why they weren't allowed up here.

We made it to the top where Sage unlocked a door, holding it open for me. I hesitated before walking in, noticing we were only in another hall. This one, however, was far less inviting than the others.

The carpet leading down the hall had been destroyed, torn beyond repair. Even the walls looked like a lion had run its claws through it, creating deep gouges. There were dark curtains over the windows, but I could tell that the glass had been broken by the way the drapes rippled from the wind.

"Is it safe?" I asked quietly, unsure whether I could still do this. I did not know what I expected, but it was not this.

"For the moment it is," Sage replied mildly, his words doing nothing to calm my nerves. He started forward but stopped when he noticed I was no longer following him.

"Rowan?" He said, looking at me expectantly.

I tried taking a deep breath and moving forward, but my legs would not allow it. They remained in place, attempting to will my mind back down the stairs. "Sage, I'm deeply sorry, but I do not think—" I started, the words leaving my mouth before I could stop them.

Sage stepped towards me as the words trailed into silence. He searched my eyes as if the answers to my fear lay within them before his hand hesitated, grazing my chin. "Rowan, I would not invite you here if I did not have faith in your abilities," he said softly, his gaze still on me.

"It is not my abilities I worry about," I hissed, pulling away from Sage and turning my back towards him. "It is whether they will work on the King. If they do not, I will be a lifeless corpse," I started, my words becoming quieter as I added, "I may not enjoy this world and some of its inhabitants, but that does not mean I am ready to leave it."

It was quiet for a moment before I felt a hand on my waist, and Sage began turning me back around. His expression was serious, his brown eyes holding sincerity. "Rowan, I will not allow any harm to come in your direction. In his own way, the King will not. He ordered me to stay within the room when you are with him, at all times. He knows I will prevent him from destroying another life. You have to trust me."

I could not tell him, but that was the problem. I didn't trust him. I knew nothing about him or who he was. He was still but a stranger to me, although he seemed to think otherwise. I had never trusted another human with my life, and I wouldn't start now with a mere guard.

When I didn't respond, he sighed, looking up at the ceiling in thought before his eyes drifted back to me. "The moment we leave that room, I will draft up a contract for your forest. I will have the King sign it this very day and announce the new set of rules. All you have to do is meet him."

My eyes flickered before they closed. "Let us go before I decide it is no longer worth it," I said, bracing myself.

"Thank you, Rowan," Sage whispered, but by the time I opened my eyes, he had already turned and began walking towards the door at the end of the hall. I followed behind after a moment, my feet dragging.

Sage reached the door and paused before knocking firmly three times. I waited for some sort of response but only received silence. Was the King in there? Surely he didn't spend all his time in the same room, so it was plausible he left.

"Perhaps he's gone to run an errand," I said to Sage, who only shot me a look before knocking once again.

"Your Highness, it is Sir Coventry. I have come back with the one who has the ability to tame even the wildest of animals," he tried but still, silence was the only one who would respond to him.

"Her name is Rowan and she has dealt with wolves—" Sage started, but a chill went through me when he was interrupted.

"Her?" Was the simple response he received, but it was still enough to scare me.

"Yes, Rowan is female. I know she was rumored to be male, however everything else about her is true," Sage responded and I frowned. I had heard all that was whispered about me, but never the suggestion that I was a male.

There was another moment of silence, and I thought that he would make us stay outside. Just as I started to suggest we try again at another time, King Sandalius spoke once again.

"Come in."

Sage glanced back at me before he turned the doorknob, and the door groaned open. He then took a step inside and, with much reluctance, I did too.

Chapter Eight

- -

Last update of the month! It'll be back to my sporadic updates, sorry! I hope you enjoy the moment you've all been waiting for ;)

The room was in the same condition as the hallways, yet it looked worse with the destroyed furniture. There was a couch that had been torn in half and a mirror with shards of glass surrounding it. A lamp stood nearby, although it gave no lighting and, judging by its stance, it no longer could.

I almost didn't see the King because I was so focused on the room itself. It was a disaster—something I didn't think even a professional designer had the ability to fix. It was beyond repair, but you could tell by the fine colors that it had once been grand.

"Your Highness," Sage said, and I looked over in time to see him bowing towards the windows. My eyes drifted in the same direction and found the reason I had been brought here.

The first thing I noticed was that his black hair was a mess. It was dark, shades darker than I had realized the color itself could be. It was also long and pulled back, although I could tell it had been a long time since it was last nurtured.

His skin was just as bad, from what I could see. It was light, much too light. I wondered when was the last time it had been kissed by the sun, and if it ever had. A doctor would find it concerning, seeing the complexity of his skin.

His clothes were faded in color as if they too had missed the touch of the sun. Parts were torn, allowing the King to blend in with the room.

Yet, at the same time, he stood out. He was exotic in comparison. He was alive with a beating heart, while everything in the room had been torn and broken. He was the last thing left—the only one standing.

His back was turned but he still said, "You can stand now Sage," as if he could see us.

Sage straightened and walked over to the King, his movements slow but his footsteps loud. I had once done the same thing with an injured possum. If I moved too fast, I could scare it and then it would harm itself further. If my footsteps weren't loud enough, I could slip up and scare it, only to result in the same thing. It was exactly what Sage was doing with the King.

"Our journey within the forest was fine, and there were no unexpected surprises. Her father has been brought to the nearby town, as you requested," Sage explained, and I blinked in surprise. I didn't think the King would be responsible for my father's living arrangements, much less care about it.

"And how is our guest?" The King responded, not bothering to glance at me. I stiffened, something Sage caught when he looked back at me. He shook his head slightly, before answering the King.

"She is fine. She has requested that in return for her services, you ban hunting and killing in the forest she resided in. I told her it would be done."

"She must have quite the personality to demand things from me," the King murmured, still not looking back at me. Sage attempted to stop me, but I didn't pay attention.

"I want protection for the animals. If you cannot do that, you can forget about my service," I snapped, nearly regretting it when the room descended into silence.

I did not think I'd ever understood the true definition of fear until King Sandalius turned around, his distinctly hazel eyes trained on me. When he began moving from his spot, my entire body froze.

It was fear that kept me from moving or attempting to find shelter from him; it was fear that caused me to forget all of Sage's warnings, my eyes never straying from the King's.

"Do you think," he started, taller than I realized. Even if I stood on the tips of my toes, I would still not be equivalent in height. "—that I will simply cave into the demands of a female?"

My head remained high, despite the need to back away. He was close now, close enough that I could see his eyes resembled those of a wolf's. They were eerie, yet beautiful.

"You will, if you desire any help from me," I replied calmly, surprised my voice did not shake as much as my nerves were.

I could see his nostrils flare at my words, his eyes narrowing at the silent challenge. He flexed his hands by his sides, as if to loosen them.

"Get her out of here before I decide I do not give a damn about her abilities," he whispered, and Sage was over by my side in a second, pulling me back.

He opened the door to lead us out, but the second he did, an orange ball hurled itself at me, chattering nervously.

Behind him were several guards, all winded. "We're sorry, he just darted inside—" one started, but it was the King who finished.

"Get out! Get out now!" He snapped, his voice like the boom of thunder. I could see him visibly shake before he grabbed the nearest chair.

I watched as he hurled it with great strength and it flew, sailing through the air before it met the wall. It was there that the chair met its end, the wood shattering and breaking off into a multitude of pieces.

Sage chose then to push me out, slamming the door shut behind us. He did not stop running until we were out of the hall, the second door also closing when we were all out.

However, even from there, I could still hear the cries of a wolf.

Chapter Nine

We were now downstairs. Sage had dragged me back to the room he said would be mine, although by his current mood, I did not think it would remain that way for much longer.

He paced across the floor, his boots thumping against the ground. I sat on the edge of the bed, watching him. It had been this way for several minutes, and I wondered if it would remain so for hours more.

"I told you." The silence was pierced by those three words, shattering like broken glass. His voice was firm, anger stirring beneath the thin layer of calmness.

"I told you I would take care of my part of our deal," he added, his volume beginning to rise. "Yet, you ignored me! Do you now see why you cannot challenge him? Would you prefer to be in the place of the furniture?" He snapped, finally halting in his movement, his eyes on me.

"I'm not at fault for the King's anger!" I snapped back, standing up. I would not sit here and allow him to scold me like a spoiled child.

"What your King needs is to leave that area! Do you not think that could be the reason for his anger at everything? He lives up there all alone, trapped like a domesticated wolf! If you attempt to keep a wild animal locked up in your house, it will eventually turn against you," I replied, my own anger slipping through.

People continuously attempted to tame wild animals, desiring exotic pets. However, when these animals began showing signs of their instinctual natures, their true selves, humans no longer wanted anything to do with them. They would feign disgust at the animal, perhaps have it put down for its "inhumane" nature.

"You cannot expect him to live up there in solitude and not change. If he is as animal-like as you say, he needs more freedom. The space in which he resides is much too small for him. Any animal would be in distress living the way he does," I said, much softer.

I looked at Todd, who had found the dresser. One of its drawers had been slightly open, thus it became an invitation to him. He was now curled inside, fast asleep. I could only imagine how stir-crazy my little one would be if he did not have the forest to run in.

"He prefers it that way, Rowan; it is not us who sent him up there. He does not want to be around so many people when he has the opportunity to hurt them," Sage explained, sighing. It seemed his anger had also evaporated.

"It does not matter, Sage. This is one way you can help him." I paused, walking past him as I opened the door and peered outside.

The hall was almost empty, save a couple of guards and a servant. For a castle as big as this one, the hall should be filled with more people.

"Are there many guards and servants left?" I asked Sage, closing the door and turning back to him.

He studied me, wondering where this was going. When he couldn't figure it out on his own, he answered: "There are not many left. They feared for their lives or their families after an incident."

I opened my mouth but decided it was best to close it. I did not think asking him what the incident was would be a very good idea. I might end up joining those who left if I found out.

"Send the remaining into town. Allow them to visit their families for a few days; I do not care what you do with them. When the castle is empty, you can take him outside into the nearby forest. This way, he does not have the chance for another incident to occur," I explained, but Sage frowned.

"I cannot do that, Rowan. If he even allows me to, which he will not, some will not have somewhere to go," he said but I shook my head.

"There's a town nearby. They can stay there and visit. They can go in groups, a guard with each of them. I do not care how you do it, but this is your best opportunity," I said firmly, watching as he clenched his jaw.

He looked at me for a moment, his thoughts fighting with one another before he finally answered. "I will talk to him," he said shortly and I nodded, relaxing.

"Good. While you are here with him, I can visit my father and—" I started, but Sage was quick to stop me.

"No, Rowan. You will be there with us; do you not understand? You are here to interact with the King so that your magic works, not to advise me. You cannot visit your father yet," he said, and I could feel my nerves fraying.

"I have helped you! I should not have to hold his hand on the way to the forest; that is your job!" I snapped back, nearly pulling my hair out of my head.

I wanted to make sure my father had settled in fine, yet Sage had other plans. If he thought I would follow as a loyal dog would, he needed to readjust his plans.

I wasn't going near the King until I was calm enough to deal with his anger again, but that certainly wouldn't be anytime soon.

"Your magic will not work if you are not around the King, will it?" Sage snapped back, and I opened my mouth but replied by biting my tongue.

I could see satisfaction cross those brown eyes before he continued. "Exactly. So you will be by the King's side, along with myself, when this plan is put into place."

"You cannot expect me to continue working with you when I am not sure of my father's health right now!" I tried, but he only began adjusting his armor, preparing to leave.

"I was told by those who brought him in that he was fine. I will check on him myself today, but you will have to wait until later." With that, he walked out the door, not once glancing behind him. Had he, he might've caught the storm in my eyes.

"This is why I easily prefer you over humans," I muttered to Todd, whose eye had lazily opened when the door closed. His gaze remained trained on me, the other eye opening as well when I sat on the bed's edge.

Within seconds, he jumped from the dresser drawer and onto the bed, chattering as he climbed onto my lap. I sighed, stroking his fur in thought. The King was certainly going to be more of a challenge than I had expected.

He was rumored to look like that of a beast: hideous and brute. Some claimed he had claws in place of fingernails and teeth as large as a leopard's. Others said he was tall enough to tower over anyone who stood in his way and was built like a bull. None of these proved to be true.

King Sandalius only seemed like a malnourished human in my eyes. His nails appeared to be bitten as far as he could go, ragged and torn. I was sure his teeth weren't equivalent to a leopard's since they all fit within his mouth, none hanging out. He was tall, but not tall enough to tower over all of his enemies. He may have been built at one point but now, he was only a skeleton of what he used to be.

I had heard of how quick his temper could turn from the calm ocean waters into screaming waves that crashed against the sand in protest. However, it was different experiencing it in person where the threat was much more immediate than the rumors.

He had attempted to control himself—which was a start, I suppose. Had he not, I might've been the one harmed instead of the chair. It showed that he wasn't a lost cause, despite how difficult it was going to be to help him.

I was almost positive that some fresh air would help his mood, if not anything else. I hadn't lied to Sage: wild animals did become stir-crazy when placed in an enclosed space for too long. What worried me was that he had been locked inside the room for so long that the approach in mind wouldn't do much else.

Going outside could become a routine thing, enough so that his skin would regain its natural complexity. The walks would be a small substitute for exercise and perhaps aid in reconditioning his muscles. They could ultimately help fix his physique; however, they could do little to nothing for his mental stability.

Todd's chattering brought me back, taking me away from my thoughts. I sighed at him, pulling him closer which he was completely fine with.

For now, the small plan I had created would do. It wasn't much, but it was something to create a foundation with that I could build upon. I would worry about how to deal with his mental situation later as I couldn't fix everything at once, no matter how much I desired to do so.

"Let us hope this works, little one," I murmured into Todd's ear before laying down on the bed with him next to me, my thoughts floating around the both of us.

Chapter Ten

The next morning I was awoken by a series of quick raps against my door. I decided against answering it, curling closer to Todd who was radiating heat. However, the knocks continued until Todd left my side, darting to the door. I sighed, knowing he was ready for his daily adventure outdoors.

"Rowan, we have to talk. It is your option whether I come in against your will or you choose to open the door. Either way, we will speak." This was said with irritation, sounding more so like a threat with each word.

"I can hear you perfectly fine," I murmured, although making no movement towards the door. I could hear him blow out a puff of air before a smile appeared on my face at the thought of him becoming frustrated.

I could hear the lock clicking, and my smile was lost as I realized he was forcing his way in. I climbed out of the bed, standing there with crossed arms as I waited. It wasn't long before the lock finally opened, the door cracking open not a moment later.

Todd was quick to scurry out the room, nearly tripping Sage on his way out. Sage frowned at him, watching the reynard disappear before making his way into the room.

"Did he agree to our arrangement?" I asked, not bothering with greetings. They weren't the reason I was here and being virtuous would not solve the problem at hand.

Sage finally looked at me, frowning once again. "Were you not aware of the clothing placed within the wardrobe? There should be both day and night clothes, all made to fit you," he said, and I bristled at the words.

I had fallen asleep in the dress, drowsy from the day's travel and the adrenaline that had run through my body upon meeting with the King. Changing had not been something I thought about.

"A question begs for an answer, not another question," I replied, watching as his eyes narrowed at my words.

"I cannot present you to the King in the same dress, Rowan. You are to change, and then perhaps I might consider telling you what is expected for the day," he replied, his voice as calm as ever. One day he would finally lose control, and I hoped to be the source of it.

He walked towards the wardrobe without waiting for a response, opening it and shifting through the clothing. I briefly looked in and realized it was stocked with clothes, all brightly colored and finer than the ones I had brought with me.

I could hear him grunt softly before pulling back from the wardrobe, a dress following along. "Put this on so that we are not late," Sage said, pushing it in my direction.

I frowned, staring for a moment before walking past him towards my suitcases. They were both there, although I had not noticed them earlier. I could hear Sage's sigh when I began to open one, rummaging through.

"Your clothes are not sufficient for a lunch. Can you not see past your stubbornness and listen to me just this once?"

I stiffened at his words, throwing a glare over my shoulder. "I am not the only stubborn one in this room. Perhaps you should consider listening to me for once. I was not informed of this beforehand, therefore I will dress as I please." With that, I pulled something from my suitcase and walked into the bathroom.

"You are going to cause my death," I heard through the door, muffled and irritated. I found a smirk playing on my face at the words, satisfied he was beginning to realize just how I felt about him.

I looked at the clothing I had chosen and smiled in thought, remembering when my father had brought it home. It had been a lazy summer night, and I had anxiously been awaiting his return. He was occasionally hassled by the people in the town; although, it had never become serious. However, it was still enough to fill me with worry.

He finally returned, and I had helped him by bringing in the supplies while he went to the couch to rest his back. I had begun placing the supplies where they belonged when he called me over, his voice elated.

I had gone over and there was the dress, lying across his lap. He had told me it was on sale and that the moment he saw it, he'd thought of me. He said I would blend in with the forest and its creatures, becoming more and more attached to them.

The dress was beautiful, and I couldn't help but think that it had been made for someone like me in mind. The dress' fabric was a variety of deep red shades, some blending together to create a black hue. The material wasn't as soft as the dress I currently wore, but it was certainly sturdy.

Whomever had delicately sewn the dress together had done so with leaves in mind as that was what the dress appeared to model. There was a single leaf carefully placed where a strap might be, with several others falling gently down the dress and skimming my calves. There was a small flower pinned in the middle of the chest area, holding it all together.

It was my most cherished item, one that I would continue wearing until it fell apart. The sight of it sent reminiscent thoughts through me, and I began to yearn to return to the forest and its inhabitants.

"Rowan, we cannot be late. It will not create the best impression, nor will it give him a reason to consider your plan."

I sighed, gritting my teeth at the words to keep my tongue in check. He would quickly learn just how much I cared about whether I was going by the King's schedule if he kept speaking.

I changed into my dress, folding the other and placing it on the counter before running a brush through my hair. I glanced in the mirror once before walking out, Sage pacing the floor as if he was the nervous one.

He glanced up when the door closed shut, his eyes studying me. I could see them flicker and I thought he would say something sarcastic, but instead he asked, "Are you ready?"

"Yes," I replied, slipping into a pair of sandals nearby. I was as ready as I could be for lunch with an ill-tempered beast.

Sage took the lead, opening the door for me. I stepped out, waiting before we began walking through the halls. "Why are we attending a lunch with the King? Is he not capable of eating in solitude since he prefers to do everything else that way?" I asked, my voice casual. It was enough for Sage to throw one of his infamous looks in my direction.

"You can continue to test my patience; however, the King will not allow you to do so for long. Saying such things around him will lead to disaster, Rowan," he started, pausing before continuing with, "He would prefer to speak with you in person about this plan and suggested doing so over lunch. He would also like to apologize for his behavior."

We were rounding the corner, closer to the room where I had first met the King. "What was the point of you presenting the idea to him if he would prefer to hear it from me? It seems like a waste of time and needlessly redundant. Were you not able to tell him all of the details?"

This time, he didn't even look in my direction. "I told him everything; he would simply prefer to hear it from you. It is the same as drafting an agreement with someone: you may have a friend present it to them, but they would rather go over it with you."

We had finally reached the door which Sage opened, allowing me to walk in first. I did, going up the stairs, and all excess noise cut off when he closed the door. We ascended in silence and I allowed him to unlock the second door, my heart-rate picking up its speed.

The hall was as ragged and torn as it had been the first time and showed no signs of changing soon. I waited on Sage to walk forward and followed behind, my reluctance growing with each step.

"I beg of you to keep your mouth under control. Please, just for this event," Sage muttered and I frowned, opening my mouth to respond. But before he could even knock, the door was opened.

Chapter Eleven

This one is dedicated to MY BEST FRIEND, Shaterria ;), whose birthday just passed. I love her more than anything and it's dedicated to her for allowing my use her name. Enjoy the chapter!

There stood Shaterria, the female whom I had briefly seen in the stables. She wore a formal dress, and I wondered whether she was dining with us. I was answered when she spoke.

"Good afternoon, Sir Coventry, Rowan. I thought the chef would have arrived by now. Come in," She said, bowing slightly before opening the door further.

It was obvious that there had been an attempt to clean up. Some of the destroyed furnishings were gone, but not all of them. There was even a wooden table placed near one of the large windows with four chairs surrounding it.

The King was close to the table, staring at the floor in thought. As if sensing someone watching, his eyes flickered in my direction, no longer unfocused. I knew I was supposed to look away, but my eyes wouldn't flee from their destination.

"Rowan, let us sit down," Sage said, his voice soft but firm. He lightly touched my hand with his and began guiding me in the direction of the table. It was then that my eyes finally fled, their attention turning towards Sage.

I could see the warning in his gaze, as if I had already done something wrong. I pulled my hand from his, muttering, "I do not need you to hold my hand. I have the ability to walk without causing a disaster."

"I am beginning to doubt that," Sage murmured back and I huffed in response, not bothering with a reply.

When we walked to the table, Sage was quick to pull out a chair for Shaterria, who replied with a thank you before sitting down. I grimaced, grateful he hadn't done so for me.

I began to pull back my chair but froze when a hand was lightly placed over mine, halting it. I didn't have to look up to know it was the King, who had moved closer without my noticing.

"Allow me," he said softly, his voice tame in comparison to when we had first met.

Instinct told me to snap that not all females were expecting a man to pull out her chair and in fact, some preferred doing so themselves. However, a single glare from Sage stopped me.

I moved to the side slightly, watching as he pulled out the chair. I glanced up and saw him staring at me, a thick eyebrow raised expectantly. He wanted me to sit down and give him my back.

I stood for a moment, reconsidering the thought of snapping at him, but it would do no good and probably keep me here much longer than I was already going to stay.

So instead, I pushed back my instinct and slowly sat in the chair, my posture stiff. I bit my lip when I felt him pushing my chair in before he finally left.

There was something about him that scared me, yet I couldn't place my finger on. It wasn't because of his animalistic side; that was the side I felt comfortable around. It was his human side that I didn't trust. That was the side that was unstable and more unpredictable than anything.

I watched as he sat in front of me, Shaterria by his side. She was looking down as if afraid to meet his eyes. However, the closer I looked, the more I began to think it was because of his behavior. Her shoulders were relaxed and her posture wasn't stiff in comparison to my own: she felt comfortable around him.

Sage had taken the seat by mine and appeared as comfortable as Shaterria looked. It caused me to wonder just how often they were around King Sandalius and how often they had witnessed his rage. One couldn't be comfortable around a man like him unless they knew how far his temper extended.

"How are you enjoying your time here, Rowan?" Shaterria asked, breaking the silence that had began to build and twist itself into another form. She was attempting small talk, something I had never found interest in.

"Tiring," I replied, not bothering with a more in-depth answer. It wasn't my job to entertain the King, nor was it my job to lie.

I could tell my answer wasn't enough from Sage's sigh and Shaterria's pointed look. I almost snapped at them, unwilling to sit in silence any longer; however, it was then that someone knocked on the door.

"I'll get it," Shaterria offered, quickly rising from her seat, walking towards the door. I could hear their hushed voices for a minute or so before the door was closed again.

I turned my head slightly to see what was happening and saw Shaterria rolling a cart in our direction. I could only guess that the chef, or guard, wasn't allowed in the room, which was why she was the one who was serving our food.

When the cart reached us, Sage stood up, preparing to help her. But she shot him a look before saying, "I'm perfectly capable of putting dishes in front of everyone, Sir Coventry." It was said lightly, but enough to draw a frown across Sage's face and a smile on my own.

I could see the King watching all of us quietly, as if studying our reactions. He hadn't shown much emotion this entire time but simply stared. In that, I was reminded of the natural curiosity found within wolves.

"I believe the chef told me that we were being served farfalle pasta with pesto sauce and roasted chicken today. Is this fine, King Sandalius?" She asked, setting the dishes in front of us, carefully and one-by-one.

The aroma alone was enough to set my stomach off. It was certainly more rich and divine than anything I had been served at home. I wondered whether my body would be able to handle such a feast.

I watched as King Sandalius examined his own plate, doing so for several minutes. I caught myself staring, awaiting his response. There was absolutely nothing wrong with his lunch, from my perspective.

When he finally responded, it wasn't what any of us had expected. "Rowan, do you truly believe this plan of yours will work?" He asked, his eyes still on the plate.

I glanced at Sage who shrugged, unsure of the King's reaction. When my eyes returned to him, they were met by a pair of hazel ones. "I do believe that it will help stabilize the wolf within you, yes. However, I do not think that it alone will fix you."

"Have you ever been near a wolf? They are truly mesmerizing. They have bonds that we, as a society, should strive towards," he said before moving his plate to the side, losing interest in what lay in front of him.

"They are beautiful creatures. I lived relatively close to a pack," I said, relieved we were conversing about a topic I was well-versed in.

"Then you are aware that wolves do not waste their time with trivial matters, correct? If a wolf within a pack is not necessary, they are killed or attacked until they leave," he said slowly, and I tensed, watching as he looked down at the food again.

"If this is a waste, it would do you well to remember that," he added before standing up. He began walking away and I watched, incredulous.

"I will not—" I started, pushing my own chair aside as I began walking towards him. However, Sage was quick, pulling me back the moment I stood.

"You are dismissed. Be sure to send the food to her room," King Sandalius added, and I started yelling but was dragged out of the room.

When the door was closed, I yanked away from Sage, my anger intensifying. I was not a subject that the King could just threaten and order around as he pleased. I would not allow someone to treat me in such a way.

I stormed out of the hall and down the stairs, Sage on my heels. He did not speak, but simply followed. I preferred it that way, as I wasn't in the mood to hear him defend his King.

I found my way to the temporary room and closed both of the suitcases I had opened this morning before grabbing them. I would not stay here, nor did I plan to help the King. He would continue down his dark path.

I started towards the door, but Sage stood there, silent and unmoving. "I will not be spoken to like that," I said cautiously.

His eyes softened, yet he didn't move as I would've liked. "Rowan, running will not solve this. He is going to request that we hunt you down and bring you back. If you run, I am positive our original agreement will become null, and your father will not be allowed to stay within the town.

Would you prefer for him to return to your home, alone? Would you prefer for the animals within the forest to continue being hunted down for sport? This option results in only disaster, Rowan. Staying here will at the very least provide benefits for you, your father, and your forest."

I looked away from him, too stubborn to see his reasoning. I cared deeply for both the forest and my father; however, I did not want to reside in a place where I would be disrespected. I had already dealt with a lifetime of disrespect and refused to do so any longer.

"Move, Sage," I said, my voice unyielding. I thought he would remain still and lock me within the room. I was proven wrong when he sighed and shifted to the side, looking at me with expressionless eyes.

"Rowan, this will do no good," he said, but I ignored his words and walked out, leaving the castle behind.

Chapter Twelve

Okay, just a small warning. I've gotten rid of my editor so it's just me again ;* I won't be looking for an editor anytime soon because I want to try going solo again. The point of me telling you this is that there's going to be more mistakes than usual, but just stick with me! I'll be proofreading and whatnot, but regarding punctuation and grammar I may be a little off. ANYWAYS I hope you all enjoy this chapter. Thank y'all for being so patient with me.

Chapter Twelve

I found my way outside where Todd was running around, perhaps looking for the mice nearby. When he saw me, his ears perked and he scurried in my direction. I opened my arms and in an instant, he jumped. Within the same moment, I could see a guard stepping off his horse, talking to a servant.

"There's our chance, little one," I whispered before placing Todd into my bag, gently slinging it over my shoulder.

I could run to the horse, hop on, and ride away. However, there was the matter of my suitcases, which would need to be tied up. I couldn't do so if it became apparent I was attempting to escape. Instead, I would pretend as if what I was doing was normal.

I walked up to the horse, head held high as I avoided eye contact. However, before I could make it to the animal, I was met by the guard who appeared as expressionless as the rest.

"What do you think you're doing?" he asked, crossing his arms. He was trying to intimidate the truth out of me, but I wouldn't fall for it. I wasn't going to stay here any longer.

"I was told my ride would be ready by now," I started, yet he didn't move. "Well?" I snapped, and he narrowed his eyes.

"Who sent you out here?" he asked, not willing to buy my story. I wouldn't give up that easily.

"Sir Coventry." This caused emotion to flicker through his eyes, and it was enough for me to continue. "Shall I go fetch him and tell of your incompetence?" It was a bluff, and a thin one at that.

We stared at one another for a moment before he finally grunted, stepping to the side. A servant who had been watching offered to tie up my bags but I declined, quickly doing so myself. It wouldn't be much longer before Sage rounded up his men to begin hunting for me.

Once I finished, I jumped onto the horse, whispered sweet words to her, and galloped away. I knew I could find the town by following the dirt path that was too loose to hold anymore grass seeds. It had been used too many times as people went back and forth from the castle to the town.

The entire time, I found myself listening closely to the land around us for any sign that we were being followed. I was waiting to hear the snapping of twigs or the crunching of leaves under the hooves of a horse; however, I could not hear anything.

I became so focused on listening for any suspicious noises that I did not realize we were close to the town until the silence dissolved, leaving behind a residue of voices. I finally began paying attention to my surroundings and saw that the path was ending, presenting a small town to me.

The people were constantly moving, all going along their daily routines. The sight of them reminded me of a factory: constantly in motion, pushing along through day-to-day activities. They were so content with one another, something I didn't think I would ever understand.

I continued along, ignoring the multiple stares I received. They couldn't possibly know who I was and were likely attempting to intrude into my business. It was yet another reason I preferred animals to humans.

The sound of hooves calmed me, keeping me centered as we walked through the town. Sage had told me my father was living on the edge of town, as he had requested, and that he lived in a two-story house.

The town was filled with small one-story houses, all neatly kept. However, the farther I walked, the larger they became. It seemed as if they were attempting to hide the houses from view, to keep others from wanting to join their town.

It was only a few minutes before I finally found a small pot sitting outside one of the houses, a budding Aconitum standing tall. I smiled faintly, knowing it was my father's. I would tell him the flower was horrid, yet he claimed it reminded him of me and continued to nurse it.

I slid off the horse, murmuring sweet words to her before tying her up on a nearby fence. I made my way to the house, lightly knocking on the door. I waited a moment, hearing nothing, before jiggling the doorknob. I continued moving, turning the doorknob all the way and stepping into the house.

I had expected the lights to be off and the room to be covered with a thin layer of dust. The selfish part of me had hoped my father was not able to live without me; however, guilt crushed the thought. I was proud of him for doing so well on his own, servant or not.

The lights were on, and the house had been decorated with small things from our home. I could see the old dishes sitting in the sink, the tattered rug lying in the connecting living room, and several pictures of us as a family.

My father was nowhere to be seen, yet I could hear the soft melody of an orchestra playing upstairs. I followed the tune, allowing it to lead me to him.

I found him sitting on a bed, humming along to the music playing from on top of the nightstand. He looked distracted, but once his eyes found mine, they lit up, his smile momentarily reminding me of when all was fine.

"Rowan, sweetheart! I didn't think you would visit yet," he exclaimed, happiness dancing through his voice. I gave him a tight smile, walking over and embracing him. It felt nice, simple, like something I had taken for granted before and never truly realized the comfort of.

"We have to go, Papa. Now, before they come," I said softly in response, squeezing him lightly before pulling back and scanning the room for a suitcase. I opened my bag, letting Todd out to look around.

"Why, sweetheart? I love it so much here!" he exclaimed, and I hesitated in my search. "Everything is within the town and there's someone to help me out. I loved it in the forest, Rowan, but here it's not as lonely."

I closed my eyes, having already forgotten that the forest wasn't as com-forting to him as it was to me. It hadn't truly been a home for him. It was something he had sacrificed so that I wouldn't become the center of trouble. Living out in the forest had provided me with a peaceful home without the drama the town gave us.

"I don't think I can do what they're asking, Papa," I said, glancing at him. I could see him study me, his smile fading and his expression growing more serious.

"Come here," he said shortly, sitting on the bed's edge and patting the spot beside him. I immediately went over, and he took my hand in his rough ones, his eyes on me.

"Rowan, darling, if you truly cannot help the King, we will leave right now. I won't question it further," he started. "However, the girl I raised was taught not to give up when there's a bump her path. She was given her mother's spirit and her father's determination, not that of a weak-willed person.

If you quit helping the King, Rowan, it should be because you do not see it going anywhere at all, not because you cannot find a way around this single obstacle."

"Papa," I started, my voice trailing off. I knew he was right, but I could not possibly help the King if he continued acting as if I was so below him.

He pressed a kiss to my hand, a fond smile on his face. "I have faith in you, darling. You are your mother's daughter after all," he said quietly, and I returned his smile before embracing him in a tight hug.

"Thank you, Papa. You've said what I needed to hear," I whispered in his ear before pulling back.

I could hear Todd growl as he dart under the bed, baring his teeth at nothing in particular. I stiffened knowing it was Sage and his men. If all went right, I would be able to leave here smoothly.

"Papa, I love you," I said, squeezing him lightly once more before heading downstairs with Todd right on my heels, his ears pressed against his skull.

I could hear a firm, loud knock on the door before a familiar voice said, "Mr. Cavanagh, we are here for your daughter. Let us in and there will be no altercations."

I took a deep breath, closing my eyes momentarily before opening the door and coming face-to-face with the man who was the reason for my stress.

Chapter Thirteen

H e looked fairly surprised to still see me there, staring at him. "What? Am I not allowed to visit my father?" I asked, deciding to take an alternate route. Admitting my attempted escape would only result in negative consequences.

Sage's eyes flickered, probably debating whether to go along with my bluff or to call me out. I looked at him, hoping he saw my willingness to try again with the King.

I crossed my arms, tapping my foot impatiently. "Well? Am I needed at the moment?" I snapped, the guards behind Sage looking uncomfortable on their horses. Sage stared at me for a second longer before turning to his men.

"You're all free to leave now; I will assist her back to the castle," he ordered, nodding to them. They each nodded back, hesitating but still obeying. I watched as they rode off, leaving us and the town behind.

"You are more trouble than you realize," he muttered, stepping into the house without asking. I bit my tongue, knowing now was not the appropriate time to patronize him.

"This is not as easy as you are making it out to be," I replied calmly, not allowing my anger to reveal itself.

He looked around the room, running a hand through his pale hair. "You cannot do this again, do you understand?" he asked, his tone tinged with concern.

I opened my mouth to repeat myself in a sharper tone, thinking perhaps it would penetrate through his dense skull that I would not obey his every wish and command simply because it was his desire.

But he rushed towards me and I found myself stepping back automatically, my back slamming against the front door. He had come close to me within the last second, much closer than I preferred.

The intensity in his brown eyes burned through me as they attempted to make me realize the importance of his words. "Rowan, he will harm you if he finds out about this. It may not be physically or directly, but it will hurt nonetheless. He will not take lightly to someone leaving the castle when he was willing to grant them permission to come inside. This does not happen as often as you seem to think," he explained, a desperate tone underlying his voice.

"He is not that easy to—" I started, rephrasing my previous statement. However, he caused me to stumble over my own words, forgetting my intention as his large hands unexpectedly encased my own. Their warmth travelled through me, coloring my cheeks the slightest.

"I believe in you, Rowan. I have not doubted you for a moment," he stated, his eyes on mine before they glanced at our hands, which he raised slightly. "These hands have tamed countless animals, more than you are aware, I am sure. They are capable of doing things others cannot fathom and turn away from. Your talent is much more powerful than you are giving it credit for."

I became quiet, softened by both my father's words earlier and Sage's speech. They both had an immense amount of faith in me, something I greatly lacked. My father believed I could do anything, but Sage was a mere stranger. He did not know anything about me, excluding the rumors that floated about. Yet, he still had faith in me.

"I will give him a chance," I started, my eyes momentarily leaving his. But they abruptly turned into steel orbs when I added, "I will, however, leave if he refuses to cooperate with everything I offer. And I will not be returning next time."

His shoulders dropped a noticeable inch at my words, a sigh of relief escaping from his lips, as if I had relieved him of a burdensome weight. "That is all I ask. I know he is not the easiest to approach or work with, but I believe your stubborn nature will come in handy for that. An unyielding woman is what crafts a man's heart," he murmured, and I frowned, the last sentence familiar.

It was part of a bedtime story children were told about a hardened woman and a tough man who changed his ways once he met her. There was more to it, but it was that line that I remembered more than anything.

My father used to tell me that my "hardened" nature was something that took time to get used to, but that a man would love me just as someone had loved the woman.

As if that's what I needed to complete my life.

"You are both going to lead me to my deathbed. I hope you realize this," I finally said, deciding to ignore his earlier words.

His mouth frowned deeply but I could see his eyes light up a fraction, as if the tension had drowned in the waters.

"That is only if you do not kill us off first," he muttered back and it was my turn to frown. I opened my mouth to snap that I was the least troublesome of the three of us, but he began talking before I could say anything.

"Where are your things? We should leave quickly before the King is aware of your disappearance." His voice had returned to holding its steel edge, remembering his formal manners.

Before I could respond, my father appeared from upstairs, Todd at his heels. "Don't forget this fox. We both know I am not up for sparring with him and his little spats," my father said, frowning at the aforementioned fox who had made his way to me, sitting beside my feet.

"I would never forget my little one," I murmured, Todd's dark eyes staring up at me, sensing the affection in my voice was for him. I returned his look with a small smile before my father began speaking again.

"Now, you'll be visiting again won't you, sweetheart? Soon, I hope. I've missed your company," he exclaimed and it was then I took my time to study him.

It had been a long time since I had seen him so relaxed, so free. The tired ring that seemed to stain his eyes had cleared away, leaving a shine of light. His smile seemed more frequent than rare. He even looked younger.

"Yes, Papa, I will visit as often as I can," I replied, walking towards him. His arms automatically opened, soon enveloping me.

He pressed his lips to my cheek, quietly whispering, "Do not let him tower over you, my Rowan. Your resilience is stronger than his anger. You are more than he realizes. Help him understand that."

I nodded briefly, appreciating his words. I would not allow the King to continue underestimating me. I was not a mere servant of his that he could turn away with the flick of his hand. I was much more and he would soon see that.

"We need to go," Sage said softly, his words hesitant. I frowned towards him before turning back towards my father.

"I will be back, Papa. I love you," I said, kissing his forehead.

His skin crinkled as he smiled at me, his words as joyful. "I love you too. I'll be waiting for you, darling."

Before I left, however, I wanted to make sure Sage and I were still on the same page. "The agreement we arranged between the two of us is still intact, yes? If I can tame the King, the forest will be unharmed?" I asked, examining him.

Sage looked me directly in the eyes as he answered, his expression unwavering. "Yes, I will keep my promise to you, Rowan. I have no intentions of breaking it." I nodded after considering his response, finding it to be satisfactory.

With that, Sage, Todd, and I headed back to the castle and back to where my most challenging obstacle lay.

Chapter Fourteen

- -

I AM NOT DEAD SURPRISINGLY. I just haven't had motivation to write, but I'm back! I have been writing for the past few weeks, but it's been a new story, which is started. It's called "melancholia" and you can find it on my page! Anyways, thank you to those of you who haven't completely given up on me just yet. I know I'm a mess but I working on it. And, of course, I hope you enjoy the chapter!

Chapter Fourteen

When we arrived back at the castle, there stood Shaterria, her arms crossed as she watched us. Her dark eyes were filled to the brim with suspicion, but Sage and I remained quiet as we rode up to her.

"What are you up to?" This question is not pointed towards both of us but stabbed directly at me.

"I wanted to see my father, so I did," I replied crisply, pulling the horse up to a stop and climbing off. I gently stroked his head before handing over the reins to a nearby guard.

Sage did the same, walking up next to me. Shaterria examined us both, the fiery look in her eyes portraying she was not yet satisfied by my answer.

"That required a mass of guards to chase after you? Sage, are you going to continue her lie for her or tell the truth?" She asked, and I clicked my tongue in response to show my distaste for her words.

Sage shot me a look before turning his attention to her. "She informed me when I found her that she was visiting her father. Rowan came back willingly so I do not see the need for alarm," he answered calmly, causing Shaterria to sigh, her dark eyes glancing towards the sky.

"I see you intend to be dragged down into the trenches with her," she started before adding, "The King requested your presence, Rowan."

I felt Sage's hand brush against the small of my back, as if not trusting me to leave. "Then we shall go," he said, nodding at Shaterria before gently guiding me towards the entrance.

However, Shaterria shook her head, placing a hand on Sage's chest. "You are to assist me with an errand. Rowan is to go alone."

I could feel the air freeze around us, waiting for chaos to strike. But Chaos remained hidden, deciding now was not the best time.

Still, Sage frowned, his light eyes holding an overcast. "I am not to leave her alone with him, no matter the circumstances. You know-" Sage started arguing with Shaterria, his voice firm.

"I will be fine. I can handle my own against him," I said, cutting their words off.

"I would have faith in you if I did not know about your attitude," Sage shot back without hesitation.

I crossed my arms, raising an eyebrow. "Then you are willing to place your distrust in me over your loyalty for King Sandalius? If you join me, you would only be disobeying and disrespecting him."

I could finally see him yield to me, hearing his sigh and the frustration within his body language. "Rowan," he started as if to lecture. But I would not hear it.

"I will be fine," I pressed, and I could see him waver.

"You need to be careful, Rowan. You may be the Tamer of Animals, but he is not just an animal. Keep that in mind," he said, the anger having drained from him as it was replaced with a mix of worry and caution.

I feigned annoyance, however, I was anything but. The few times I had been with the King had not gone well and I did not think it was wise to go alone. I knew animals, but humans were still a mystery to me.

The King had requested to see me alone and that was how I would meet him. I would not allow him to think I did not have enough strength to visit him alone or that he had control over me. That was something that caused deaths and vicious attacks in the wild.

So I would go alone and convey that I was not scared or intimidated by him in any way.

"I am not as dense as you seem to believe. Run your errand and find me when you return. We have to prepare for the King's departure into the woods," I said, before turning and walking into the castle.

I thought it was best to leave my things inside the room I was residing in. If I had to run, I did not want to stumble while holding my things. I then head there, Todd restlessly chattering in my ear.

"I know, little one," I start as I open the door, walking into the dark room. "You're free to roam about in a moment."

Todd's chattering unexpectedly turned into low warning growls and I froze, my hand hovering over the light. Someone else was in here.

I switched the light on, turning to find someone sitting on the bed, hazel eyes watching Todd and I. Todd's growls grew into snarls and I could feel him struggling to get out of the bag. His senses told him that it was a predator that sat in front of us.

"Enough," I snapped, gently taking him out the bag and bringing him into my arms. He calmed his snarling into silence, however, his fur bristled in every direction, his ears were flat against his skull, and his eyes never left the King's.

The King's eyes were now solely on Todd, seeming to have forgotten about me. The moment the King's mouth opened, Todd's own did the same as he bared his teeth.

"He looks as if he has been through his fair share," the King murmured, studying Todd who was a ball of fear and energy by now.

"What do you want?" I asked, ignoring his words. I was not interested in side chatter with a man who I wanted nothing to do with.

His eyes were still on Todd as he asked, "Where did you go?" The question was simple, yet I could feel the warning it contained.

"I went to visit my father, as I'm sure you know. You are wasting both our time by asking pointless questions," I replied, and his hazel eyes turned away from Todd and landed on my own. I stiffened, remembering Sage's advice of avoiding eye contact. Yet, once again, I found myself unable to do so.

It was incredible, how much his eyes resembles those of a wolf. If I did not see the pale skin that shaped itself over his skull, I would not notice a difference. The whites of his eyes were not visible, only the yellow coloration looking at me. It was what gave him the same wise, endless stare of a wolf.

He watched me for a moment and I thought perhaps we would stay like that, but he then abruptly moved off the bed, advancing towards me. He walked slow with intent, like a predator stalking its oblivious prey.

Todd's growling returned at the movement, his muscles bunching together within my arms. I pressed my lips against his ear, soothing the both of us as I said, "Hush." The growls subsided into grumbling which was enough for me at the moment.

I also thought he would stop sooner rather than later, but he did not. He continued walking until he was close enough to Todd and I that Todd began snapping in my arms, uncomfortable with the idea of a predator so close to him.

"If you lie to me again, Rowan, you will soon learn why the castle is void of humans," he said quietly, the threat clear despite Todd's audible aggression.

I bristled at the threat, beginning to feel as Todd was. King Sandalius was doing exactly as before, however, I would not allow it to affect me in the same manner. I would not leave, not yet. I would show him that he was not the only dominant one here.

"I will not scare off easily," I said, determination an anchor for my words.

King Sandalius simply laughed at my words, unaffected. The sound was off somehow as if he didn't laugh very often. It was soft yet echoed throughout the whole room. "I've already scared you off and have yet to do anything," he replied, his expression hardening.

For that, I had no response. I had left, with every intention of never returning. "Am I not standing here right now? I've returned, that is more than most can say," I said after a moment, my eyes never leaving his.

His hazel eyes flickered at my words as if considering them. They softened with confusion before I was shut out by the expressionless face I had seen before. "Will you stay is the question at hand. How many can say that out of hundreds, hmm?" He asked, his voice causing a chill to run itself across my spine.

With that, he moved and slipped behind me, my back now turned towards him. I gritted my teeth, knowing I shouldn't have given him my back. Yet, he had moved too quickly for me.

As if reading my thoughts, he paused after opening the door, saying, "You should never give your back to someone. That is when they attack."

And then, he was gone.

Chapter Fifteen

I apologize for any errors. Enjoy the chapter!

Chapter Fifteen

The castle was unusually quiet, the only sound the inhale and exhale of the air surrounding me. Not a soul was to be seen, everyone having taken off as told. It seemed colder than usual as well, the atmosphere frigid and frosted.

I was told to wait downstairs until Sage returned from directing everyone out of the castle. Shatteria was upstairs, preparing the King for the departure. The day appeared to be a slow, unproductive one, yet today more would happen than ever.

I could hear footsteps although I had not bothered to turn. Todd was sitting beside me and had begun chattering, his ears perked as he walked in the general direction. The only person he had taken a liking to here was the person I was waiting for.

"Are you ready?" he asked, his voice as tranquil as ever. He kept walking until he was by my side, Todd at his heels.

"As ready as I will ever be," I replied, watching as my little one rubbed up against Sage. Sage too looked down, kneeling as he ran his hand through Todd's fur.

"Perhaps he should be outside," he said, looking up at me expectantly. I frowned, offended. I was not stupid enough to allow him near the King, knowingly.

"Todd is not a dog. He comes and goes as he pleases. He will leave as we go upstairs. It is as he always does," I responded and started walking forward, Todd following in suit.

As expected, once we reached the stairs, Todd disappeared. I smirked at Sage who simply glared at me before opening the door. We ascended, both of us quiet. The tension had begun showing itself, warmly greeting us.

We had reached the hall and Sage hesitated, turning towards me. "I want to thank you, Rowan," he said, startling me.

He sighed, running a hand through his hair before he began explaining. "Without you, King Sandalius would not have a chance. He would have spiraled himself deeper into his darkness until it was all he could see or until his heart stopped beating.

Yet, today gave him hope whether you are aware or not. He would have never agreed if he truly thought there was not a chance that this might help him. You are the reason he may began reversing his destination down this dark path."

That was how he saw it, I supposed. However, there was more to it in my eyes. "Sage, it is not I who you should be thanking, but yourself. I would not be here without you, would I?" I asked, and he frowned at the question.

"No, however–"

"I would have left with my father if you had not come for me, would I have not?" I pressed, and he sighed.

"That is not the point," he replied, and I shook my head.

"No, Sage, that is precisely the point. You are the savior of your own King, not me. You are as true and loyal as any knight can only dream of being," I said, watching as his expression became a tender one.

He started forward, his body closer to mine than ever. I could feel the fabric of his uniform brushing against my dress, firm and light. His brown eyes stared into my own, as if searching for something. Perhaps he found it because he leaned even closer, only a wisp of air between us.

Just as quickly as the moment had begun, it ended at the sound of a door opening. Sage was quick to fall back, the air returning to my lungs. There stood Shaterria, her hands on her hips as she studied the both of us.

"Are you going to just stand there? We don't have all week," she snapped and proceeded to walk back into the room.

I could hear Sage clear his throat, but refused to look in his direction. "It is time," he said, his voice deeper than I had become used to.

With that, he walked down the hall, leading us into the room. Once we walked in, I could see Shaterria standing next to the King, her hands folded together.

The King was dressed differently today. I thought his clothing could only get better, but I was wrong. Today he wore a white shirt that looked as if it had been worn down past its use. It was now a faded grey, holes gaping every inch or so. He also wore a pair of dark sweats that looked to have once been soft but now seemed rough.

His hair was as usual, however, still in need of care. King Sandalius' back was turned towards us, although it did not matter. I was sure he had heard us enter and was proven right when he began speaking.

"I did not think you would show," he said casually, his eyes still looking out the window and not towards us.

"I told you I do not scare easy, did I not?" I replied and heard a sigh in return. It had started, the daily, silent bickering between Sage and me.

I shot him a glare before I continued. "If you expect people to leave, then they will do just that. Perhaps it would be in your interest to think otherwise."

The room was quiet for a moment before Sage snapped at me. "Rowan, hush!" he barked, then bowed his head. "I am sorry, Your Highness. Rowan does not mean-"

King Sandalius dismissed his words with the wave of a hand as he finally turned towards us. "All is fine, Sage."

His eyes then directed themselves towards me, a smirk playing on his lips. "Rowan seems to believe she is more likely to gain my respect if she plays the dominant female rather than the docile one," he said, walking over to us.

My body tensed, but I kept my eyes on his, refusing to give in. I would not allow him to think he had any power over me. He was not my King, nor was anyone else.

"Allow me to help you," he murmured, close enough that he leaned down towards me, his body towering over my own.

"Your attempt is more likely to get you snatched up by a wolf than it is to aid you."

It took everything in me not to snap at him. I knew it would only end disastrously and perhaps with someone hurt. And it was more likely that I would be than he.

So I took a deep breath and replied, "You are anything but a wolf, Your Highness. Wolves are more than just their appearance, and you have none of that."

His eyes flickered at my words, and he stared for a moment. For once, there was no snapping or cruel words. His eyes did not appear harsh or cruel. They appeared curious.

He finally leaned back, his eyes leaving mine. "We should leave now or we will not make it back before the sun goes down," Shaterria quickly said, jumping in.

Sage appeared relieved by the lessening of the tension and Shaterria's addition. However, the harsh look in his eyes told me he was not pleased with my actions.

"Lead the way," King Sandalius said, allowing Shaterria to step forward.

We had decided it was best for her to lead while I stood next to the King and Sage fell behind. We did so until we reached the castle entrance, pausing there.

Shaterria turned, waiting for the King's permission. His eyes were squinted as he looked up out the windows above the door where the light shined through.

The King nodded, and she slowly opened the door, the sun eagerly greeting us like a pup. I could see the King shield his eyes, unused to the direct contact.

"This is where I leave you," Shaterria said, holding the doors open as we all stepped out, the air turning warm and friendly.

"We will return before the moon comes up," Sage explained, saying parting words to her before she closed the doors, staying in the castle.

King Sandalius was incredibly calm for someone who had just stepped outside for the first time in years. His body was still; however, his eyes were not. They touched everything in sight, like a child at the markets.

"The forest is this way," Sage said, now guiding us. We walked slow, allowing the King to take in all his surroundings. He was quiet as he did so, yet his expression seemed lighter than before.

Once we reached the forest, he seemed to relax. It was a place he knew and had once been familiar with.

"It looks different," he said, his eyes studying the place he had once called home.

"Just as our towns grow, so does the forest," I replied, walking forward. I had missed nature, more so than I realized.

I ran my hand along the rough bark, a reminiscent feeling running through me. I yearned my own forest now more than ever, yet it was nowhere within reach and would not be for quite some time.

"You will return one day," Sage said softly, as if reading my thoughts.

I simply looked back at him before saying, "Let us go."

As we walked through the forest, the King became more and more curious. He would kneel down and run his hands through the grass as if greeting an old lover before stroking the leaves of a tree. His eyes would save the twigs or nearby foliage or the way the dirt appeared looser in certain areas.

The animals were aware of his presence, and I was sure he was aware of theirs. When we would get close, the birds would stop chirping and any prey would still, pausing in their daily routines. All knew of the predator only a distance away from them.

"I used to roam the forest for miles and miles. Yet, I cannot remember a thing we did. All I remember is running," the King said quietly, his voice holding a nostalgic feel as he stared down the dirt path, his eyes glazed over.

I smiled briefly at his words. "Todd and I used to watch the wolves run through the forest as they passed us. They would follow the prey's migration, leaving us for the season before coming back the next."

The King's posture had relaxed considerably since we had left. He already looked more lively, his skin soaking up the much needed sun. His eyes seemed brighter as well, their hazel hue animated more now than ever.

We traveled for a few miles before Sage talked. "It is time we leave, Your Highness. It is too much of a risk to be out much later," he suggested, but the King simply shook his head.

"A little longer," he murmured, reluctant to leave the forest and its inhabitants. I understood his desire and selfishly sided with him, although I knew it was not for the best.

"The hunters will be out soon," Sage pressed, his voice firm.

The King laughed and replied, "What will they do, Sage? Shoot the King?"

Sage did not find it as funny as he did and neither did I. It was a huge possibility, considering others were not sure what their King even looked like. It seemed he had forgotten that he had not been into the public in very many years.

No sooner than that, I could hear a twig snap before something whistled through the air, slamming into a nearby tree.

*Side note: Would y'all be interested in holiday cards this year? I did them last year, and with them came an exclusive chapter for whichever ship from whichever story you wanted. To this day, those chapters still haven't been posted on here.

Chapter Sixteen

Sorry, I had a hard time writing this chapter so there was a little wait. But I've finished the next chapter as well. A lot has gone on recently so I apologize for the lack of updates, as usual. I hope you guys still enjoy!!!

Chapter Sixteen

Chaos is a man of moment. He blends in with the crowd, as normal as you and I. You pass him and smile or perhaps do not even realize he's there. He does not allow anyone to see through his veil until the time is precise.

It was then that he appeared. What once blended in with the crowd was now larger than you, louder than your eardrums can handle, and more powerful than your mind could fathom. He was surrounding you, more than you could manage.

It was then that Chaos stopped strolling among us and revealed his true persona, the hunters shouting nearby.

Sage was quick to react, yelling, "Down!" But it was too late.

The King's once calm demeanor changed as he growled, the sound as authentic as a wolf's own, his body still.

Where the King had once stood there was now a black-furred wolf, slightly bigger than average. Sooner than my mind could process the situation, the wolf sprinted away, disappearing.

"Damn it," Sage snapped, running a hand through his hair.

His eyes found mine before they widened as if something was wrong and he muttered once again. "Sit down," he instructed calmly, walking towards me.

It was not reasonable to sit down when we had just been shot at with an arrow, yet my body listened to him, leaning against a nearby tree.

"I will be right back, do not move," he instructed, once again glancing at me before running off in the direction of the hunters.

For the moment, the only sound was that of my breathing, loud and echoing throughout my eardrums. Time seemed to be moving slowly, as if I would never run out of it. My vision had become blurry, everything blending in with one another.

Sage finally returned, a worried look in his eyes. He knelt down closer to me, talking, but I could only see his mouth moving, the words hidden.

He was then moving once again, taking off the upper part of his uniform. It was odd seeing Sage in a regular shirt and to find that his face wasn't always hidden.

His hair was much paler than I remembered when I met him the first time. The hue was between that of white and blonde, a beautiful blend of the two. It was tied back, appearing fragile on such a resilient man.

He began talking once again, yet the words were still lost upon me, sinking away.

He then started taking off the thin shirt, but the action did not seem out of place. I could see that Sage's years of working as a knight had paid off physically.

His body was toned, firm yet I imagined it to be soft. His torso was a piece of art that had been carved by a perfectionist, defining lines separating each ab. I found myself wondering what it would be like to trace each line and recreate him.

He knelt down towards me, crouching with his shirt in hand. Once again, he talked, yet it was a soundless noise that escaped his lips.

No sooner than my thoughts ended, my world exploded. Everything came back into view, my vision and hearing sharpening, along with my mind. But what was the first to return was the pain.

My teeth had clenched themselves, holding back a cry. What I hadn't felt at first was now revealing itself tenfold, Sage's shirt pressed tightly against my side and held there by his hands.

"You fell into shock while I warned the hunters off. You were hit, Rowan. I need to take you back, now," he explained shortly, his eyes on mine.

I shook my head, refusing to leave. "The King-" I started, but he was quick to interrupt.

"I will worry about him later. I will take you to the castle, and Shaterria and I will find him," he added before he guided my own hands to the shirt switching them out with his.

I held the shirt in place, refusing to allow him to roam alone. "I was merely grazed. I will be fine. By the time you take me to the castle and come back out, anything could happen to the King. We have to search now," I reasoned.

I watched through his eyes as he struggled with an internal battle, neither side seeming to give in. Sage's lips turned into a frown as he asked, "I do not suppose you would be willing to wait here while I look for the King?"

I shot him a look before he sighed, standing up, his back turned towards me. It was then that I realized he was half naked, appearing much more intimidating to me in this form.

"Put on your uniform and then assist me in getting up," I muttered, my cheeks heating up before I looked away. I had more to worry about than what was currently happening in my mind.

Sage listened without argument, showing that there was a first time for everything. I could hear rustling as he placed on his uniform before he cleared his throat, alerting me that it was okay to turn around.

I did, thinking that he appeared somewhat odd now in a full body uniform. I frowned, ignoring my thoughts before taking the helping hand he had offered.

The pain soared from my side, blossoming throughout the rest of my body, piercing every nerve along the way. I hissed, my eyes closing momentarily as I stood there, unable to move.

"Rowan, please wait here. It will be quicker and less painful for the both of us," Sage whispered, his voice holding concern. He seemed to be closer than before, his words tickling my ear.

I waited a moment before answering, the pain subsiding slightly. "I will be fine. Let us go before something else happens," I said, glancing as Sage long enough to see the disappointment in his eyes.

"If you show any signs of slowing down, we are to return to the castle," he said firmly, and I nodded, exhaustion already beginning its course.

We started through the forest, Sage and I calling out for the King every now and then. Sage claimed that we were walking slow in order to completely cover the land, but I suspected it was more for my benefit.

It was not long before the sun's warmth was gone, replaced by rain that grew stronger with each passing hour. Sage had started moving faster, and I kept up, not allowing him to know that it was taking a toll on me.

I could tell Sage was worried for the King's safety, as he became frustrated as time passed, the King nowhere in sight. However, Sage appeared concerned for me as well, checking in every now and then, inspecting the wound. When he did, he would suggest that we head back which I would counter with reassurance and irritation.

But now, I was exhausted. The pain was gone, my whole body feeling numb. It was beginning to become difficult to move, much less walk in a straight line. I had done much more tasking work than this, but never while wounded. Sage caught on after a while, peering at me through the rain.

"I am fine," I tried, but he shook his head, cursing softly. He looked around us, taking my hand and pulling me a little further, veering off of the path we had taken.

After a moment he stopped, both of us standing under a thicket of trees, less susceptible to the rain and its attack. "We will rest here and continue looking in the morning," he explained before he took off his helmet, his hair still bright even in the dark.

I did not respond but leaned against a tree, slowly sliding down. The pain sparked, reminding me that it was not yet gone as I made my way down, attempting to ignore its threats. It was going to be a long night.

Sage sat next to me, his shoulder pressed against mine. "If we are not back by mid-day, Shaterria will have others look for us. I will have them take you back," he said, as if that would make this all better.

"I am fine, Sage, do not worry so much," I said softly, the annoyance nowhere to be seen. I felt it, yet I could not conjure up the strength to transfer it into my words.

He was quiet for a moment, so quiet that I thought perhaps he had already fallen asleep. However, when I tilted my head towards him, I saw that he was staring out into the forest.

I watched as he ran a hand through his hair before he turned to me, his eyes flickering before they held a tender expression. "I worry about those I care for, Rowan. Try to sleep before the sun rises. We will start our search again then."

He then turned away, his face tilted up, his eyes closed. I continued watching him for a while, with an unusual curiosity and confusion, before I too attempted to sleep.

Chapter Seventeen

S HIP NAMES for Sage and Rowan, thought of by the beautiful Jane-licious: Rage, Sowan, Saan, Roge, Rogan, Sagan, Sawa, Sawan, Roage and Swan (thought of by Luciano_Obsesser) SHIP NAMES for the King and Rowan will be in the next chapter because his first name is revealed in this one! Enjoy, lovelies.

Chapter Seventeen

When Sage finally woke up, it was due to Todd climbing on him, pressing his snout against Sage's person in search for food. I had long been awake, unable to sleep for more than an hour due to the discomforting pain.

He appeared startled at first, but a brief smile found its way onto his face as I laughed, watching him hand my little one a small piece of meat.

"Do you not know what they say about feeding strays? They will not leave if you continue doing so," I teased, watching with tired amusement as Todd stayed by Sage's side, his eyes full of hope.

Sage ran a hand through Todd's fur while Todd chattered happily, thinking he would receive an award after. When he did not, he trotted over to me, chattering a storm as if I could convince Sage to hand him more.

"Do you feel well enough to continue?" Sage asked, looking me over before he crept closer to inspect my wound.

This time, however, I pushed his hand away, frowning. "I am fine; I do not need your constant intervening. I will survive a simple graze," I replied, causing his eyes to narrow as a glare was shot my way.

In truth, I did not want to remove the shirt from the wound. I did not want the pain to return in full again and thought it was best to leave it be until we returned to the castle where medical aid would be provided.

"We can leave now," Sage said, standing up and putting on his helmet once again. I moved slowly against the tree, the rough bark scraping against my back as I attempted to get up. Todd seemed to notice and chattered louder, gaining Sage's attention.

"Hush," I snapped, Todd quieting instantly but not leaving my side. He circled my legs anxiously, waiting for me to return to the ground.

"I was going to assist you," Sage muttered, startling me as his arm unexpectedly wound around my waist, quickly pulling me away from the tree and against his body.

I could feel my heart jumping from my chest to my throat, threatening to soar out of my mouth. I refused to look up, allowing my eyes to rest on his shoulder. I had never known that contact with another human could be so intensifying.

"Are you okay?" Sage's voice was a whisper, yet it still echoed around just the two of us, causing me to jump slightly. I wondered whether his heart was trying to escape as aggressively as mine was.

It was Todd who brought us back, nipping lightly at my heels. I quickly pulled away, Sage allowing me to before he looked at anything but me.

"Yes, I am fine. All is well," I said, finally replying to the question he had asked. He then cleared his throat, smoothing his uniform before nodding.

"Good," he said, and began walking. I hesitated before following, allowing my heart to calm its stirring.

We were walking for a few minutes when Todd, who had tagged along, growled lowly, the bright fur on his back standing still and alert. I put a hand on Sage's shoulder, telling him to stop before we both listened.

They were quiet creatures, beautiful yet silent. It was why we did not hear her until we could see the gray pelt that covered her body, her large, yellow eyes standing out. They stared at us unyieldingly, as patient as ever.

She stood like that for a moment, as if waiting on us. When neither of us moved, she turned her back towards us, walking away slowly.

"We should follow her," I murmured, reaching down and pulling Todd up to me. Just like that, the growling stopped, but his eyes remained on the wolf's retreating figure.

"There are no wolves left in this forest. They were all killed off," Sage whispered back, seeming confused. I, however, was excited. I felt more at home than I had since leaving my own forest.

I started towards her, but Sage pulled me back, a frown on his face. It never seemed to leave him, always returning when I was present. "We are not following a wolf into the forest. You may be familiar with animals, but they are still dangerous," he said firmly, but I simply shook my head.

"You are more dangerous than she is," I muttered, pulling away from him and following the wolf's path. I could hear muffled footsteps behind me, reluctance in their every step.

She led us, never once turning back to make sure we were keeping up. It was not until Sage heard the rustling of leaves nearby that he stopped us, looking in that direction. Before he could even speak, I shook my head.

"That is the wrong way," I said, hearing his familiar sigh. He was doubtful of the animal, but I did not believe it was a coincidence that this wolf had crossed our path.

He paused for a moment, considering his options before saying, "Do not stray far. I am going the other direction. I will not continue following a wolf that is likely leading us nowhere." I rolled my eyes, offended by his words.

"Wolves are intelligent animals. You, however, would not know that because you do not know what intellect is. How could you when you have none of it?" I snapped, seeing his eyes harden before he muttered something and turned to leave.

Todd knew the wolf was a predator, as he had back at home. When I would walk with the wolves, Todd would refuse to join. He did the same now, running towards Sage's direction and abandoning me. I did not question him, knowing I was lucky my little one had travelled this far with us.

I huffed before returning my attention to the direction where the wolf had headed. But she was nowhere to be seen.

I walked faster than before and listened closely, but I could not find her. The only sights around me were the silent trees and meek bushes, the wind whispering to the both of them. I had lost her and I could not risk going much further for fear of getting lost.

It was then that I looked closer and realized that it was quiet, much too quiet. Even the birds had stopped their daily talk, not a chirp to be hear. I could not hear the rustling or scurrying of either the predators or prey. I then realized that perhaps I was not as alone as I had thought.

Lying there, covered beneath a rotting log, was a naked man curled against himself. He appeared to be passed out, no sign of moving anytime soon. I hesitated before walking towards him, my steps slow.

His hair was all around him, hiding his face, as if a raven's feathers had fallen off and been scattered. His skin was pale, and I would have assumed he was dead if it were not for the even movement of his chest. His body was much more lean than Sage's, which had consisted of more muscle.

I knelt beside him, carefully brushing his hair aside and meeting the face of the King's. His eyes were closed, his eyelashes longer than my own. He appeared peaceful when he was asleep, younger. It was as if all his years of pain and isolation had disappeared.

"King Sandalius," I whispered softly, so as not to startle him. He did not respond verbally, but I saw his body move in the slightest.

I ran my fingers along his face, tracing his hairline before my fingers found their way down to his jawline, feeling it tense underneath my touch. "King Sandalius, it is Rowan," I said, my voice a little louder than before.

When I did not receive a response, I started to pull my hand away. I was startled when his hand shot out, encasing my wrist, halting any movement. I stilled, adrenaline running through my veins, unsure of what would happen.

"Do not stop." His voice was ragged and hoarse, as if he had screamed into the night until the moon departed. His eyes were still closed, but I imagined them open, as drained as his voice was.

"Please." This was added as he let go of my wrist, allowing me movement once again.

That is how Sage found us, with the King lying there while I ran my hand along his face and through his hair.

Sage was quiet as he took off his uniform, stripping down to nothing but a pair of thin sweats. I started to look away, but Sage thrusted them in my direction, looking at me with his expressionless features.

"For the King. I do not think he will listen to anyone but you at this moment. Have him change so that we can return to the castle," he explained. The moment I took the uniform he walked off, disappearing out of sight.

I returned my attention towards the King, whose hazel eyes had opened and were staring at me without wavering. I watched him for a moment before placing the uniform in front of him.

"You heard Sage. Change so we can leave," I said, beginning to sit up but the King was quit to stop me.

"Wait," he said quickly, a hand curved along my waist. I felt my cheeks redden at the movement, wondering when all this unnecessary contact would stop. Between Sage and the King, I had experienced enough physical contact for a lifetime.

"Do not leave. Wait here," he said and I frowned, shaking my head.

"You are naked. I am not watching you change," I replied, relieved I had managed not to see all of the King's body.

He did not hesitate as he said, "Then turn around. I did not ask you to watch." At this I glared at him, gritting my teeth before I turned around, looking towards the forest.

I could hear the dirt and fallen leaves rustle underneath his weight as he stood up. It was a few minutes before he was dressed and he tapped my shoulder.

I turned, laughing at how ridiculous he appeared, but immediately re-gretting it when I was reminded of the pain that shot through my side, lingering as an unwelcomed guest.

"Were you hurt?" The King asked, frowning as his eyes landed on the shirt that was still against my side.

"I will be fine," I replied, standing up. It was then that the world began to darken, the adrenaline running out of my body, and everything hitting me at once.

He was by my side in an instant, supporting the weight that I seemed unable to carry. "You cannot possibly walk back. Why was she not taken back to the castle?" The King questioned, disapproval in his voice.

"It is my fault. I tried to persuade her, but she does not listen to others well. I told her that we would return if you were not found before mid-day. That was the most that I could get her to agree with." I could hear Sage's frown and the harshness in his words that was more than likely directed towards me.

"I will carry her-" Sage started, but I was quick to interrupt, having drawn up the last of my strength.

"No one will carry me or anything of the sort. I do not need help," I snapped, less energy within my voice that I had predicted. I realized my point was not coming across well, as I was still leaning against the King.

I moved away slowly, biting my tongue to keep myself from giving in to my exhaustion and pain. "See? Now let us go," I said, attempting to move them along. I sensed it would not be long before my mind gave into my body and I would have no choice over whether I was carried or not.

They both watched me warily, but it was the King who appeared as if he was about to object. He opened his mouth, but before he could get a word out, I began walking forward, not waiting to see if they followed.

The walk back to the castle appeared much more tasking than it was walking away from it. It also seemed to take longer, my every step weighing more and more than the one before.

I could hear Sage and the King conversing behind me, the King threatening to pick me up whether I objected or not. But Sage would quiet him, telling him that it would do more harm than good. For once, Sage and I agreed on something.

When we arrived at the castle, there were guards surrounding it. They were running one way or another, gathering things together and readying horses. It was not until one spotted us and yelled at the others to halt that they stopped, watching us.

"Tell Shaterria she is needed to take the King upstairs," Sage started, already beginning to direct everyone. They listened without hesitation, glancing back at us every now and then.

Shaterria came out quickly, rushing over to us. "Your Highness, are you alright?" She asked, inspecting him. The worry in her voice was clear, her eyes as wide as a deer's.

"I am fine. Take Rowan and patch her up," he said, looking over at me. I frowned, shaking my head.

"I would prefer to patch myself up, thank you," I said, Shaterria looking me over with a pointed look before she persuaded the King to allow her to assist him in going back to his room.

He frowned, glancing once at me before I could hear him say, "Go back downstairs after and make sure she is well and patched up." Then he and Shaterria were gone.

"You cannot shut everyone out."

I did not turn to look at him, but merely crossed my arms. "I have done a sufficient job of doing so. I did not have any problems until you came into my forest," I shot back, walking towards the castle.

Sage did not leave me alone as I had hoped, but followed me. I headed into my room, opening one of my suitcases. I had brought along an aid kit my father had made, thinking perhaps I might need it. I had been proven right.

"If you shut everyone out, then who can you trust or fall back on?" Sage asked, leaning against the doorway as I pulled out the kit.

"I do not need to be dependent. There is such a thing as being independent, Sage. I have done fine," I scoffed, sitting on the bed.

Sage walked over to me, sitting beside me, the kit between us. Before I could grab it, he snatched it, smirking. "What you are is prideful, Rowan. There is a difference," he said, opening the small kit.

I crossed my arms, looking over him. "I am in a dress. How do you expect to help me?" I asked, watching as his confidence slipped from his face as his eyes traveled over me, realizing I was right.

But instead of leaving, he simply went to my suitcases and pulled out a pair of shorts and a shirt. They were both more faded than not, often used when I went into the forest to assist my father in his daily work.

"Change," he started and when I did not move, he added, "I will not leave until you do so." He then turned around with the kit in his hand while the clothes were laid out on my bed.

I sat there for a moment, looking at Sage's back. He was odd. They said the more you get to know someone, the less they surprise you, but I did not feel that would be the case with him. He was different than the humans I had been around my entire life. I did not know if it gave me hope or simply terrified me.

I decided it was best to listen, rather than disobey. It would only cause more bickering and I believed that Sage would not leave the room until he had his way.

I gently took off the dress, making sure to do so more carefully around the wound. It was a slow process- taking off the dress and replacing it with the other clothes- but I eventually finished and sat back down, redirecting my attention to Sage.

I cleared my throat before saying, "I am decent. You can turn around." He turned, his eyes studying me before he walked over, sitting so close that I could feel his the fabric of his pants brushing against my bare leg.

"Hold your shirt up while I clean the wound," he instructed, gesturing towards the mentioned area. I did as told, making sure to hold it high enough so that I would not be in his way.

The moment Sage saw the wound, a frown formed and his eyes turned a shade darker. "Why did you not listen and go back to the castle when told?" He muttered as he opened the kit, rearranging it before pulling a few things out.

"If I left you would've-" I started, but the second he pressed an alcohol soaked wipe on my skin, the words dissolved, momentarily forgotten as I hissed, biting my lip.

"You should have listened. Perhaps you would not be in so much pain," he replied, the satisfaction in his voice poorly veiled. He pressed it against my skin once more, his eyes only softening when I flinched at the contact.

"Perhaps the only reason I am in pain is because you're here," I replied, narrowing my eyes at him. I would not admit that he was right, although I did not regret my decision.

He simply shook his head slightly, his blond hair falling around him as he leaned down, taking a closer look. My hand twitched, the urge to run my hands through his hand running strong. I wondered whether it would feel like the fur of a large cat, which he reminded me so much of.

"Your prideful nature will hurt you one day, Rowan. I only hope that someone is there and brings you to the realization that isolation is not the only option," he murmured, his face still hidden from my view.

I opened my mouth, but inhaled sharply as the needle pierced my skin, distorting my thoughts. I gripped the sheets, looking anywhere but at the Sage's actions. Just the feeling alone had caused my face to pale and my hands to shake.

"Rowan?"

I had not realized that time had passed, or that Sage had finished handling the wound. I looked down and saw that there was now a white gauze placed over it, the needle gone.

I glanced at Sage, whose eyes were studying me, as if questioning my actions. "Are you afraid of needles, but not strange animals?" Sage asked, his studying rewarding him when I grimaced.

"We all have a weakness. I can usually avoid mine," I snapped, daring him to press it.

He sighed, watching as I folded the torn dress and put the kit back in my suitcase. "Had I not been here, would you have left the wound to get worse? If you could not watch me, then there certainly was no way that you could have patched yourself up," he shot back, his voice laced with disappointment.

"I would have found a way. It is not for you to worry about. You can leave now and attend to your priorities," I said, walking towards the door and holding it open before pointedly looking at him.

He just stood there for a moment, his brown eyes on mine, and then walked out, pausing to say, "Do you truly think isolation is the best answer? The King believed as you did and now he as far from humanity as he can be. Do you think turning into someone so controlled by impulses, so unable to control their emotions, is the best option?"

And for that, my mind held no answer.

Chapter Eighteen

- -

Ship names for the King and Rowan are: Kierowan, Rowan, Kieran, Kien, and Krown all provided by the incredible Luciano_Obsesser! I hope y'all enjoy the chapter and have been doing well!

Chapter Eighteen:

The next few weeks were similar in comparison, excluding the excitement of the hunters. At the end of each week, we would request that everyone in the castle leave. There were, of course, no complaints for fear of the King's wrath.

Sage and I would then leave with King Sandalius, Shaterria staying behind to take messages brought while we were away. She would ask to come along from time to time, but every time it was decided that she would stay behind. Sage promised she would be allowed when the King was more stable and that he would be the one to stay behind.

The walks through the forest were longer each week, the King demanding to stay out for a while more. Sage would attempt persuading him that we should head back before the moon rose, but it was useless as the King never listened. When he was finally ready to leave, the moon would accompany us on the way back, in the lead.

King Sandalius' changes were only now becoming noticeable. Where he had once appeared coiled and hardened, he was now alert and calculating. His skin had become a few shades darker, eagerly soaking up what the sun had to offer. Even his movements were less stiff and more natural, walking with authority.

He would sometimes shift into his wolf and run ahead of us, causing an endless amount of stress for Sage. However, before the day ended, we would locate him and he would shift back appearing more relaxed than ever. Sage had gotten into the habit of bringing along an extra pair of clothes for him.

Now, the King was speaking quietly to Shaterria at the castle doors while Sage and I waited outside. Sage had worn his uniform for most trips, but he would occasionally wear just his pants and a regular shirt with a vest, as he was doing today.

It was odd seeing him without the helmet, his hair tied up in a bun. It seemed I had forgotten there was a man underneath all the layers he wore. Even the King appeared different, wearing a shirt with less holes than usual and a pair of dark jeans. His hair was also tied back, but in a ponytail.

I, on the other hand, was wearing a pair of shorts and a shirt that I wore while working in the forest. My hair was tied similar to the King's as it would frizz throughout the day and become a nuisance if I did not do so.

The King's talk with Shaterria ended, the doors closing behind him as he joined us. The King led the way, Sage and I following behind as usual. Todd joined us occasionally; however, he steered clear of the King most of the time. Today he was nowhere in sight, having left earlier.

We had begun walking and were now in the forest, getting farther away from the castle. Even now, the King still ran his hand along the trees, bushes, and everything he could. It pleased me to see someone appreciate nature and all of her beauty.

"Tell me about our home."

I glanced towards the King, who had not turned in our direction when he asked the question. He was looking up at a tree, where upon closer inspection I noticed a bird's nest lay. The mother was quiet, even her chicks silencing their crying for the moment.

"It is a small house in the middle-" I started, but he shook his head, a frown settling.

"He means your home, Rowan. Your forest," Sage supplied, his body turned to me. His own eyes were filled with curiosity, as if the subject interested him as well.

I shrugged, walking towards the tree where the King stood. "Back up," I murmured, looking once at the King. He hesitated, as if he wanted to object, but he did as told and went near Sage.

"My home is my own little world," I said softly, looking up at the bird's nest. I could see the mother perched on the edge, looking down at me. She was a beautiful painted bunting, her dark eyes contrasting with her brightly, multicolored feathers.

"At first, it was simply a forest. I had not met a single animal there." Birds were often unappreciated, no one realizing what intelligent animals they were. I had perhaps been one of those people, but that had long ago been altered.

"And what changed that?" Sage asked. I did not have to look back to know he was studying me, watching my actions.

"My little one did," I said, a smile forming on my face. The mother's eyes were still on me, her head tilted. I reached into my bag, pulling out a small packet of seeds I had brought along during each trip.

"When I first encountered Todd, it was raining very badly. I would not have noticed him if his fur were a shade darker. But there he was, lying underneath a few small plants. I thought he was already dead."

I held out my palm, the seeds spread. It was quiet for a moment before she flew down, gliding neatly onto my hand. Her beak was gentle against my palm, easily snatching up the small seeds.

"It was hard taking him home. He would growl and snap the moment I approached him. I stayed outside with him for an hour before he finally gave in and let me touch him. My father was surprised, of course, but he helped me nurse my little one back to good health."

I reached towards her slowly, feeling her flinch when my finger lightly brushed against her. I waited a moment before touching her again, however this time she simply ignored me, eating once again.

"I did not think there was anything special about it because people take in injured wild animals all the time. However, it was a bit odd that Todd turned a bit feral when my father tried to tend to him but remained calm when it was me. We simply decided that he had become attached to me because I was the one to find him.

When my little one was all well, I knew he was not better off left alone in the forest. Even if I had tried, Todd followed me around everywhere like a small pup. It was around then that I noticed the squirrels would stop scurrying up trees when I approached."

The bunting had finished the food and she sent a chirp my way before she flew back up to the nest, returning to her young. I murmured parting words to her before glancing back at the King and Sage.

They were both staring at me, but it wasn't as the town had done. There was no disgust or even fear in either of their eyes. They did not cringe from me or look down as if I was not worth their time. They merely seemed surprised, both refraining from speaking.

"I have been bringing along small snacks for the animals. I knew one day they would begin to trust me so I decided to try today. It is easier to gain the trust of the prey rather than the predators," I explained, looking away. I did not enjoy the staring, as it was usually accusatory.

"I cannot imagine an entire forest filled with animals that do not shy away from you," the King said, his voice calm as he walked past me and took the lead once again.

Sage took his spot beside me, walking in silence before he decided to speak up. "I think the King is becoming used to you. He has not been curious about anything in a long time. You are making progress, Rowan," he said, veiled happiness in his voice. He was happy that his King was returning.

"We," I said, not looking at him. "I have not been alone in this, Sage. If it were not for you, I am sure the King would have killed me by now and his own health would have deteriorated further. We are making progress."

It was quiet for a moment before I could hear his soft voice whisper, "Thank you." I would not admit it, but the smile in his words had brought a brief smile to my own.

It was erased once we reached the King, who stood still, his head looking down at the ground. Next to his feet, there lay a body as still as ice. I too froze, but Sage rushed over, kneeling down. I watched him check for a pulse before he lightly cursed.

I had known he could not be alive. His head was tilted upwards, his eyes left to glance at the sky for eternity. His mouth was gaping open, blood smeared along his lips. Later, it would be told to us that his tongue was missing, having been torn out.

He wore a white shirt, similar to the King, but it had been torn into shreds, barely intact. His chest has been clawed open, the gaping wound almost theatrical. The marks were none other than claw marks, similar to those left by a predator, such as a wolf.

"We need to return to the castle and report this incidence," Sage said, standing up. His face was expressionless, as dead as the day I had first met him. It was apparent that he was accustomed to Death and her ways.

The King did not respond, still staring at the body. I walked towards him, and it was then that I noticed his eyes were not as expressionless as Sage's. They held the most emotions I had ever seen in them. His eyes were filled to the brim with a gruesome mixture of fear and worry.

"King Sandalius, we are to return to the castle. They will find out what happened. I am sure it was no animal," I said, placing a hand on his upper arm.

His eyes flickered to me at the contact, as if he had not heard Sage and I approach or speak. "We must go," I repeated, gently pulling his shirt in an attempt to lead him.

We returned to the castle, King Sandalius remaining close to me the entire time. When we returned, Sage rushed to Shaterria, murmuring a few words to her before coming back.

"Take the King upstairs. Shaterria and I will deal with the incidence. It is best the King is not seen when the Council comes to investigate," he said and I nodded, watching as he turned and disappeared from sight.

I took the King upstairs, both of us walking slowly. He was quiet through-out it all, not having spoken a word since asking me about my home. I was surprised, not expecting the death of a human to stir him so much.

"At home, there were deaths within the forest," I told him. We were stand-ing next to the window, the King looking out while I watched him.

"However, each was determined to be an act of murder by humans or just a human provoking a scared animal. Animals do not attack unless given a reason. I am sure all will be fine," I told him, hoping to bring some reassurance.

I sighed when he did not reply, prepared to give up. Just as I turned to go, he spoke.

"Rowan, it is not the animals' lives I fear for. It is my own," he said, his voice much lower than usual.

I could feel unease building inside my bones, the tension slipping into the room. "I have been going to the forest during the week, alone. There are some nights-," he paused, the tension pressed against us both, waiting for the chance to fill the entire room and kill us.

He took a deep breath before starting up again, his next words lowering the temperature within my body. "There are some nights where I do not remember what happened, when I have come back covered in blood. It is possible that I killed the man."

A Thank You to You

This is NOT an update, nor is it really anything pertaining to the plot of the story. It is simply a thank you to all of you. If you've read Property of a Gordon or His Experiment, you may be familiar with this. You're free to skip this, but skim the bottom and see if you're username is there because it may be!

So for this thank you, I want to make it stand out from the others, as I don't want each one to just sound like I copy and pasted them, or that I don't put my heart into these.

I'm a very introverted, insecure person but I've been attempting to work on that. I can't begin to list all the things that I don't enjoy or like about myself, but the one thing that I'm confident about is my writing. This is 100% because of y'all.

I've enjoyed writing since I was a little girl, but it wasn't until I joined this site that I felt I was actually good at something. I begin to branch out and finished not just one, but four stories. I've made countless friends that I wouldn't trade for anything and I feel because of the confidence y'all gave me, I feel a little more confident in my day-to-day life.

I've been told that my stories have affected some of y'all in one way or another, but I just want y'all to know you aren't the only ones being affected. You have all affected me more than you can ever know and for that, I cannot thank you enough.

When I wrote this story, I really thought there would be backlash for Rowan's attitude. I agree with Rowan on the whole human-animal thing, but I don't tell people that, ever. So I decided to share my thoughts through her. I am more than thrilled, and surprised, to say that there has not been a single person who's been offended by Rowan's opinions. There have been several people agreeing wholeheartedly with her, and I'm amazed.

Of course, I have to thank you guys for putting up with my awful updating schedule. A lot has been going on with me, and I lost motivation to write. I thought it was best not to force a chapter, knowing I would be disappointed by the results later and end up disliking the overall story. But, hopefully, I can do better as I have a small outline ;)

Thank you for allowing my to voice my opinions and Rowan's. Thank you for allowing me to introduce you to a fox who's devoted to his person, to a guard whose loyalty is endless, to a messenger who can take care of herself, and to a King who is both man and wolf.

This story has, by far, been my favorite to write. I love the bickering between Sage and Rowan, the tension between her and the King, and of course her little one. It's a joy to write this story, and even more of a joy to read your comments, or see your usernames pop up on my phone when you vote for a chapter.

It seems a lot of you are between ships, unsure of who to pick which just shows I'm improving, luckily. Property of a Gordon, little of you chose Nolan (I was team Nolan DESPITE HIS FLAWS), and Patience of a Gordon, it was a little more divided although I believe more were for Prince Gordon. Originally, in His Experiment, I wanted there to be a love triangle between Varian Arcelia, and Him, but I realized that He was too cruel for that to happen.

This is all over the place, so if you've made it this far thank you for bearing with me omg. Thank you for clicking on this story, for adding it to any reading list of yours, for reading even just the first sentence, for reading all of it, for voting for this story, and for your beautiful comments. Thank you for not giving up on this story, or me, Thank you for allowing me to never doubt my writing, and for being there for me more than you can imagine. Simply, I want to thank each of you for being yourselves and having faith in me.

I'm going to apologize in advance because I already know I'm going to forget names. PLEASE PLEASE PLEASE post a comment and tell me if I've forgotten about you. These are in no particular order:

Shaterria: Some of you may know her as Shay from Property of a Gordon. If you read the comments before the chapters, she called you her f"ing peasants, which most of you went along with, as she was definitely joking. Thank you for allowing me to use your name in this story and I love youuuu.

Brunetiquette: MY BOO, MY LOVELY!!! You already know I love you. Thank you for letting me bounce ideas off you and for being MY FRIEND. Thank you for skyping me and keeping me company. Thank you for always making me laugh and cheering me up. Thank you for believing in me and so much more.

xcyson: Thank you for helping me by editing the first 12 (?) chapters of this story and for being my friend and for skyping me all those times. They all meant more than you know.

Luciano_Obsesser: THANK YOU for your hilarious comments and for providing me with ship names. I always end up laughing and enjoy our small little conversations in the comment sections. You've made my day/night more than a couple of times.

Mush_Puppies: Thank you for your enthusiasm in every single chapter. Thank you for always providing funny comments and for providing me with motivation to write.

Janelicious: I think you're in ever thank you note I've written xD You've basically been with me since the beginning which is crazy to me omg. Thank you for all your comments, our talks, making me laugh, for ship names, and sticking with me. It means so much to me.

KimTracey: I saw you have another account now (I assumed it was the same person omg)! You've also been with me for a while, which means so much. Thank you for your beautiful comments and not giving up on me.

LadyTokimi: Thank you for your wonderful message on my message board. I love getting messages on there and it means a lot that you're enjoying Rowan so far. Thank you for giving this story and chance!

Galip99: Thank you for sharing your thoughts about Rowan on my message board. I was thrilled to hear someone thought like her and that you loved Todd. He's my fav ;)

YourAlteza: Thank you for all your wonderful comments, for staying with this story and its journey, and for your patience <3

Samandalee: You've also been with me for a while, so thank you for sticking with me and for every comment you've shared. Thank you for talking with me several times. You mean more than you know to me.

Mikrikuklitsa18: Thank you for all your comments and for making me laugh. Thank you for providing insight on the chapters and for letting me see how a reader thinks.

RoseNymph: Every comment you've ever left has beauty and grace in it. They're always beautiful and warm my heart, so thank you.

GloriaAkowauh: Thank you for everything you've done. You've been with me for a while as well and mean more to me than I could ever express.

lostinWonders: Thank you for your votes and for also speaking with me multiple times. I've enjoyed your company and hope all is well with you.

Nightlytimes, Zozo593, vikacloud, Razza_, and fandoms_4_fangirls, Farah_bananabee, Blessed_07, DreamingSheWolf: Thank you for each of cour comments. They have made me laugh, smile, and appreciate my writing a little more with each new one.

TyreshaLovee, Puppyloveraylin, ofstardustandscars, jhow333, lismo2, bamagranna, fangirl565, lanarogers, goodtobealive, intoxicatewonderland, staythenight, waywithwords7, snor16, acaciaforshey, blackonei, purplerayne99, -marirose-, trina1010, stylesrule, wolfclaw2004, flawlessflower_, these-lovely-bones, Alchemist_, miss_periwinkle, Ali_just_a_writer, sweetlima, as560312, august_rush15, foreveranasian, bonniem1998, soft_gray, kittiekitkatz: You've all voted on this story maybe once, or multiple times. You may have also left a few comments and I cannot thank you enough. I love you all and cannot express what you mean to me.

The Silent Readers: I can't see y'all but I know you're there. I don't expect votes or comments and am thrilled that you're reading the story. Thank you for giving my story a chance and for providing me with your silent presence. I appreciate y'all so much and love you. Thank you so much for being there and sticking around.

The Voters: I don't have a feel of you guys, but I still love each and every one of you. Some only vote on one chapter, others on some, and others on all. You guys are always the first to read an updated chapters and the last.

I'll see a vote within less than a minute of updating and it makes me smile. So thank you.

The Commenters: As always, I will share my opinion that y'all are a crazy bunch. Your comments range from being filled with an immense amount of love to flipping in a second to a threatening vibe when a character does something you don't like. It's the funniest thing to me. You all make me laugh, tear up from happiness, and smile. You guys are my motivation, my muse. I love getting a chance to speak with you about the story, and sometimes, about yourselves. I love having a chance to get to know every one of you. So thank you.

Chapter Nineteen

- -

I apologize in advance for typos and allll that. BUT I knew I wouldn't be home for a while where my laptop is so I decided to update anyways. I hope you all enjoy!!!

Chapter Nineteen

"Papa, where are the eggs?"

"Behind the milk!" This was shouted from upstairs before I could hear his footsteps descending.

I checked, and there they were. I had decided to make food for my little one since the two of us were staying with my father this weekend. Todd wasn't pleased, but I refused to let him run around in a town with strangers.

He currently sat patiently at my feet, his head tilted up as he watched my every movement. It was as if his stomach was never-ending. I leaned down, running a hand down his back before my father joined us.

I pressed my lips against his cheek, frowning down at Todd when he bared his teeth. "You are not being nice. Enough," I scolded, watching his mouth uncurl before he tilted his head innocently at me.

"I am sure he will settle down once he's fed," my father said, chuckling before he walked to the small wooden table and sat there. "How have things been, sweetheart?" he asked, a thread of caution hidden in his words. He knew something was wrong, as he always did.

"Fine, Papa. It is nothing for you to worry yourself with," I replied, focusing on Todd's food.

I could hear him sigh before I looked over and saw the small shake of his head. "I'll always worry about you, Rowan. You are my greatest treasure; have you not realized that by now?"

I loved him more than anything, but I knew once I told him of the incident at the castle, he would insist we leave. It was different seeing the lifeless body lying there rather than just hearing about the numerous murders.

"How is everyone treating you? Do you enjoy it?" I asked, hoping to catch him off guard. I was proven successful when he face lit up like a star, a grin taking over his face.

"It's wonderful, sweetheart. The town's people aren't afraid of me nor do they treat me any differently. There are events every week that Lily and I attend-" he started and I raised an eyebrow, glancing at him.

"Lily? Is she the one sent to watch over you?" I asked, making sure that there was someone sent to watch over him. It was part of the agreement and I had not had the time to properly introduce myself to her or make sure she was okay.

"Yes, she's lovely. She's quite different from you. Has the patience and ease that you never seemed to grasp," he teased, showing all his teeth. I smiled at his joke, laughing.

Had anyone else said it, I might have snapped about where they could take their negative comments. However, I knew my father did not mean it harshly. He often told me that my temper and stubborn behavior were an advantage, not a disadvantage.

"Ahh, you must be enjoying the contrast. Has she been taking care of you? Has she been helping with the daily chores, going to the market-" I was cut off as he walked over to me, hushing me.

"Rowan, you don't need to worry about me. Lily helps as much as she can. However, I am still capable of doing some work by myself. Do not spend your energy worrying about how I am. I have never been better," he explained, his words tugging at my heart painfully.

I knew if I asked, when everything was done, my father would leave here without question and return to the forest. He would do so because of me. But would he be happy there when here there were people to talk to, things to do, and places to go? Would he want to settle for a quiet forest where there was no one but Nature?

"I am glad you enjoy it here, Papa. Perhaps I will be able to worry less knowing that," I said softly, giving him a small smile.

I feared that soon we would be leaving the town, my services no longer being needed. If the King believed he killed the man then there would be no need to try helping him. They would finally kill him as they had been hoping to do for so many years.

It was rumored that the only reason the King was not dead was because the Queen had put a stop to the death sentence, despite King Sandalius pleading and begging to have someone end his life. She had said he would not be killed as her husband had. She wanted to give the King a chance to make up for his mistakes by giving him a "pass," so to speak. Since then, she has disappeared and the King has reigned over the lands.

Yet, knowing this, I would not tell my father. It would be wrong to ruin his happiness with the news that we would be leaving soon. I did not want to see him hurt in any way and I certainly did not want to be the cause of it. He had been through so much, sacrificed so much for me, that he deserved this happiness and so much more. I was already dreading the moment we did have to go.

"How often does Lily come by? Will I see her this weekend?" I asked, hoping to clear my mind. If I strayed too far, either Todd or my father would notice and begin to worry too.

He smiled at the question, answering, "Yes, today in fact. I invited her over to have dinner. It's a pleasant surprise to know you'll be joining us."

We talked some more while I fed Todd, who happily dozed off in my arms after. It was not too long before there was a knock on the door, my father's face etched with confusion while Todd stirred, grumbling.

"I didn't expect her until later," he explained and I stiffened, placing an annoyed Todd on the ground before telling my father that I would answer it.

Todd followed along, a sign that perhaps it was not danger that lay behind the door. I paused, taking a deep breath before swinging the door open. What I had expected was a council member or someone of equal grimness.

What I had not expected was a man dressed in a buttoned-down white shirt and black pants. His hair was tied in a ponytail today, the sun's shine bouncing right off. In his hands, he held a bouquet of flowers.

"Who is it, Rowan?" My father called from the other room while I frowned, opening the door and allowing our guest in.

"It is only Sage, Papa," I called back, closing the door behind him. I looked expectantly at him while he studied his surroundings, not saying a word to me.

I opened my mouth to speak, but my father walked into the room, greeting Sage. "Hello, Rowan has said so much about you! Are those flowers for her? Did she tell you that sunflowers are her favorite?" my father said, laughing when I shot him a look.

"Hello, I came by to visit your daughter and thought it was only suitable to bring you a gift of sorts. They are from the castle's garden, where the most valued flowers are grown," Sage said, offering the roses to my father.

My father beamed at the gesture, more touched than Sage knew. My mother had grown a small garden outside of our house and once she passed away, my father had tended to it. Flowers were a weakness of his, no matter the type.

"They're beautiful, and quite large too. Have you been to the garden, Rowan? My, you must tell me about the flowers," he babbled, placing the flowers in the vase while openly admiring them.

I focused back on Sage, who was paying attention to Todd. Even though he had just eaten, Todd's front legs were on Sage's, his snout pressed against Sage's pocket as if he were trying to dig out whatever was there.

"What it so dire that it could not wait until the weekend?" I asked, watching Sage pull out a small piece of meat and hold it out to Todd. He didn't wait a second before snatching up the meat, pleading Sage for seconds.

"Enough," I said, watching Todd grumble before heading out the room.

My father re-entered the room, an apron tied around his waist. "Will you be joining us for dinner, Sage? There will be plenty for all four of us," my father asked, thrilled that he was cooking for more than the two of us.

"No, I will not. I apologize, but I have duties to return to at the castle. Perhaps next time," Sage said, a soft smile on his face. I relaxed a little, relieved he treated my father with respect.

"Nonsense! It won't be long and this way, you are filled up for the journey back. I'll set a plate for one more," he said, talking more so to himself than to Sage and me. I sighed, laughing softly as he walked away, muttering and setting up another spot at the dinner table.

Sage looked confused, unsure of what had happened. "If you truly need to leave, he will understand. Now will you explain why you came here in the first place?" I asked, my voice low. My father did not need to know what was going on.

Sage nodded, glancing out the window. "I cannot be long for there is a storm coming. However, I felt it was important to tell you that the council will be here when the week begins. They will expect to speak with you about this situation and about what we have been doing," he explained, studying me.

I looked away, frowning. "Sage, I do not think I am a credible source when it comes to the council. If a town filled with people did not trust me, why would a council built to protect those very people believe a word I have to say?" I asked carefully, hoping he would see reason.

"You do not have a choice in the matter. If you do not speak with the council, you will be punished for inaction and they will believe you are protecting the King. In reality, both of us are not sure what happened. It would be best to provide our statements rather than be silent and provide guilt.

You simply have to answer their question as straightforward as you can. Do not add on detail as you may provide them with something they can twist to fit their needs. They will try to confuse you and look for anything to use against the King. We cannot let that happen, do you understand?"

I was silent for a moment, the intensity of the situation slipping onto my shoulders and lying there, gaining more and more weight with each passing second. This was not supposed to be easy in any sense, yet I had not expected anything this drastic.

"I am familiar with how it works," I said, already exhausted from the process. Sage's eyes flickered with questions but before he could press me, there was a light knock on the door, signaling our last guest.

Dinner was pleasant; my father enjoyed the company. He and Lily spoke through most of it with Sage and I joining in on occasion. Todd had settled himself at my feet, chattering softly as if to throw in his opinion. None seemed to notice the decline in my mood.

"Papa, I will do them. Go sit down," I instructed, taking the plates from him. "Enjoy your guests. Allow them to compliment your cooking," I teased, hearing his laughter before he thanked me and left the room to join Sage and Lily.

I put up the leftovers before washing the dishes in a spaced-out state. It was a very meditative process, repeating the same thing over and over, allowing my mind to wander to other things than what was in front of me.

It was not until someone hand brushed my upper arm that I realized I was no longer alone. I looked over, spotting Sage who now held the towel I was going to use to dry the dishes.

He began drying them silently and we both worked like that, neither of us saying a word to one another. It was somehow still comfortable, reminding me of the silence that lay between the animals in the forest.

It was then that the lights flickered before darkness surrounded us completely. I could hear my father reassuring Lily, sharing past memories of the countless times the lights in our house had dimmed out.

"I think the storm arrived early," my father said, laughing before he lit a candle, the lone flame dancing to its own beat.

I could hear Sage curse lightly under his breath before we both thought it was best to join them in the living room.

"Is your horse going to be okay?" my father asked, looking at Sage.

He nodded, although his expression still appeared troubled. "She's been placed within a stable. I walked the way here."

My father nodded before sitting down next to Lily, talking quietly to her. Sage and I still stood, as if the lights would turn on soon and we could resume as we were.

"Is Shaterria at the castle?" I asked, wondering whether the King would be fine.

"Yes, I made sure someone was with him while I left. However, she was to deliver messages when I got back and I was to watch over the King," he explained, looking off into the distance.

Sage was the type that did not like when things did not go as planned. I suppose I was too, and perhaps that's why I understood his frustration so well.

"All will be fine. Whoever was to receive the messages will understand that the storm was too bad. The King will be fine in Shaterria's hands. Do not worry too much," I said, catching his eyes after my words.

They softened, his shoulders lowering just a fraction before he sighed, running a hand through his hair and tensing once again.

"Why are you not in uniform?" I asked, studying him. It was always odd to see all of him and not just bits and pieces.

"I try to avoid it while I can. I have been told that I make people nervous when I am wearing it," he explained, a grin forming on my face.

I laughed softly at his words, startling him. "I am sure you make people nervous even when you are not. It's not the uniform, Sage. It is you."

He did not get mad or offended at my words, but instead, the ghost of a smile formed. Even his eyes seemed to light up in the dark, for a moment forgetting his worries.

We all talked lightly, waiting for the storm to calm. Even my little one joined, eventually curling up beside me and falling asleep. However, by the time the moon rose for his performance, the thunder still boomed and the lightning still flashed in vicious attacks.

My father spoke first, "I suppose it will continue all night. Rowan, you and Lily can take the two bedrooms. Sage and I-"

I shook my head, cutting him off. "Papa, do not think about it. Your back will only get worse if you sleep on the floor. You and Lily can have the rooms. I will sleep on the couch. I do not mind," I said firmly, daring him to object. Luckily, Sage spoke.

"I will sleep in here with her. I will not let harm come to her. And if she is not comfortable, I will tell you," he promised, comforting my father with his words.

My father objected weakly, but in the end, he slept in his room while Lily slept in the guest room. A layer of blankets were on the floor for Sage, while I had my own on the couch.

"Do you need the candle anymore?" Sage asked, standing beside it, his body illuminated by the flame.

I was not sure he could see me but I shook my head, then given an answer when he leaned down and blew out the candle before settling on the floor.

It was quiet, the storm brewing in the background. "It is just like the forest," I said quietly, remembering the nights we spent together in the tent outside.

"I think you perhaps are in a better position than you were in the forest. I am the one on the floor," he replied, his voice surprising me. It was light and teasing, something I did not expect from him.

"Oh?" I said, a smile in my voice. "Do not think you are playing the heroic knight who saves the damsel in distress. We both are. I chose the couch instead of a bed and you chose the floor."

He laughed, the sound soft. "Yes, but you are not on a hard surface."

I huffed, silent for a moment before an idea clicked in my head. I took my blankets, moving from my spot on the couch and finding the floor, a spot next to Sage.

"What do you think you are doing?" he asked, the humor gone from his voice.

I settled down, laying with my head turned away from his. "We are equal now, so hush. Now we are both heroic knights."

"Your father-"

"He will be fine. Hush," I started, smiling briefly when I felt pressure against my back, something wet pressing against my arm.

"See, even Todd is fine with our arrangements," I added, feeling him curl up pressed against my back.

"Goodnight, Sage," I said, closing my eyes and falling into a familiar rhythm.

It was not long before I heard him reply, "Goodnight, Rowan."

Chapter Twenty

When the sun rose, Shaterria alerted us that the council would be arriving earlier than expected. I said my parting words to my father and Lily, letting him know that I would visit again soon.

I packed my things, joining Sage on his departure. I rode with him as we followed Shaterria back to the castle, all of us riding in silence. The mood was somber as if it too was dreading the return to all that waited for us.

When we arrived, it became clear that the council had made it before us. In the front, tied to a post, were several large horses, all covered in thick, silver armor. They were unswayed by the guards moving around them and the servants scurrying one way or another.

We dismounted, Sage telling a nearby servant special care instructions for Sequeria to whom he murmured goodbye, promising to see her again soon. We then headed inside, Shaterria leading the way.

"We will all be allowed there at the beginning to each tell our version of the story. However, once this is done, Sage and I will be told to leave. They were very reluctant about allowing you to stay, Rowan, but decided it was the best solution for their own well-being." She glanced back at me once, waiting for a nod of confirmation before continuing.

"They will pressure him and try to confuse him. You are there to keep him calm; however, they will be watching you too. They'll be making sure you do not help him in any way," she said and I frowned.

"If I cannot speak to him, how am I of service?" I asked as we paused in front of my room, Sage opening the door.

I stepped in, placing my suitcase on the floor and leaving it unpacked as before. I placed my bag next to it, letting Todd out. He started for the door but I stopped him, deciding to keep him nearby until the culprit was found. He was smart, but not smart enough to outwit a determined killer.

Shaterria was slow to speak, thinking her answer through. "You will be allowed to speak to him, but your answers cannot guide him in any specific direction. You must be careful or you too will be thrown out. This will be difficult. If you cannot do this, either myself or Sage will stay behind instead."

I opened my mouth to answer, but it was Sage who spoke. "She will be fine. If she cannot do it, no one can." His words were clear and firm, not once wavering. He then turned towards me, adding, "I believe in you, Rowan. You have what it takes to make sure all is right with the King."

It was reassuring to hear him say that. His words brought newfound determination to me, although I was still unsure of how it would play out. I did know, however, that I would try my best to help the King.

I nodded to him. "Thank you, Sage," I said, my voice holding sincerity. He mumbled something in return, but it was awkward, showing he was still not used to receiving gratitude.

Shaterria led the way, taking us towards the stairs where the council awaited our arrival. I stood behind Shaterria and Sage, but it did not keep the lead council member's eyes from catching my own.

"Is this who you've brought to tame the King—Rowan?" he asked, scoffing as if he couldn't believe that they would do such a thing.

Shaterria and Sage glanced at me, both looking a bit surprised. I frowned, ignoring their looks. "I am glad to see you are well, Council Member Warren," I replied calmly, refusing to give in to his childish behavior. It would not help me any, but cause harm instead.

He narrowed his eyes at me, knowing of my attitude, having spent so much time in the forest. "What is this? Where has the stubborn woman gone? Is that all you have to say to me?" he asked, causing the others to laugh. They too knew of my behavior, but I gritted my teeth.

"Shall we?" I asked Shaterria pointedly, looking at them. She was quick to nod, unlocking the door, leading everyone upstairs.

Sage and I were the last ones, giving him the perfect opportunity to question me. "How do you know them? Were you in some sort of trouble?" he whispered, trying not to catch anyone else's attention.

I glared at him, knowing he couldn't see it in the darkness. "It is not any of your business," I replied, but paused before adding, "Sometimes, deaths occurred in the forest. They were quick to blame me before blaming the animals. Each time it was ruled as the fault of the hunter, not the animal. However, it did not stop them from endlessly questioning me. They believed I killed anyone that came through the forest. It was one of the many rumors that spread throughout the land."

He was quiet, not responding. I supposed he knew better than to say he was sorry as if it was his fault. He also knew not to try comforting me. For that, I was grateful.

We arrived to the hall, the council members murmuring to one another when they saw how gruesome it appeared. If they did not enjoy the sight of the hall, they were certain to be disgusted by the room. But I kept quiet, secretly enjoying their discomfort.

"Rowan, come," Shaterria said, beckoning me over with a hand. I listened, walking towards her, glancing once at Sage who nodded in return.

I stood beside her, studying her as she stiffly said, "You are allowed in before us all. You will have five minutes with the King. It is to make sure he is stable before the council enters. Make good use of it."

She unlocked the door, allowing me to step in before shutting it behind me. I glanced at the door once more, wondering whether I was truly going to be able to do anything. Would I have been just as useful outside with them?

My eyes caught the King sitting at a table, staring at me. The room had been tidied up a bit, a wooden desk placed near the large windows, a chair for the King to sit in. There were several others in front of it, three for the council members and two other to the left for Shaterria and Sage. What I assumed to be my own chair was behind the table right next to the King.

His face was as expressionless as usual, leaving me to believe that he did wear an expression but it was his own. One that showed nothing yet still exuded authority and resilience. The King had truly mastered the look, showing no fear.

I walked towards him, noticing that his attire was different. It was not as formal as the council members, who were dressed in newly made suits. However, it lacked the usual holes and his shirt was a buttoned down one.

Even his hair had been cared for, appearing a little cleaner than before and in a ponytail.

"How was your visit home? I apologize that it was cut short," he greeted, his eyes leaving mine once I took my seat next to him. The two chairs were placed close together, little space between the King and I.

"It was fine. How are you doing? Are you prepared?" I asked, more concerned with talking about his current situation. It was possibly life or death for him, yet he did not seem to care. He was calm, much more calm than I could be.

"I will be fine once they leave. How many times did they visit you?" he asked, once again turning the attention away from himself and towards me.

They had visited multiple times, each for a different reason. From bodies in the forest to claims that I was turning the village's pets and livestock against them, I had been the primary suspect of them all. But each time, I was left alone, the councilmen disappointed and still suspicious.

"Enough for a lifetime," I replied, not going into details. I was sure he already knew the answer if he was asking, as I had never mentioned their visits to him.

"You know to answer with as little as possible, yes? If it is a yes or no question, you answer with just that. They will twist your words if you answer with more," I instructed. I was sure Shaterria had already warned him of what to do and what not to do. However, it did not keep me from asking.

"Yes, I was told of how to reply. And were you given instruction on what to do if I become enraged?" he asked, tilting his head towards me. He was merely curious, wondering if I had a plan.

"No, I was not," I replied, realizing that I had no idea what would happen in that situation. They expected me to calm him but did not give any suggestions on how I was to do so. Perhaps I was just to act as a barrier, but would become bait if anything happened.

He was silent for a moment, studying me before speaking once again. "Then you should hope for the best outcome for the councilmen and yourself." It was stated casually, as if it was not a warning but a mere fact.

We sat quietly for the remainder of the time until the others entered in, the councilmen following behind Shaterria and Sage. They looked around the room in wonder, disgust, and fear. They were viewing an exhibit that they had now become a part of.

Shaterria showed them to their seats, Sage finding his own. He looked at me, his face expressionless but his eyes holding worry. Was he afraid for his dear King? I would be too, given the circumstances. For King Sandalius to walk away clean, we would all need some sort of miracle.

The room grew quiet, sound replaced with tension. It appeared we were all in for a long day.

Chapter Twenty One

I hope you lovelies enjoy!!!

Chapter Twenty One

I was proven right once again. It was a long day already, and it was far from over.

Each interview was conducted in the room; however, when interviewed, we were taken to the opposite end of the room and turned so that we could not make eye contact with one another.

The council had begun by questioning Shaterria, the easiest of us all. She was not there, so she did not have much to tell. It was when we arrived that they were interested in, attacking her with question after question. Once finished, she was told to leave before they began questioning Sage.

He handled each one cooly with the same reserved look, giving away nothing. He did not rush his answers nor hesitate. He did not grow angry at their accusations towards the King but answered just as he had with the question before.

I was next. They questioned my every whereabout and my every answer. However, this was not a first time for me so I did not give in to their redundancy. I answered with the shortest answer, keeping my replies simple. When finished, I could see Council Member Warren's face etched with annoyance, satisfying me. He wasn't receiving what he wanted, which was clear evidence indicating that the King was guilty.

Next was the King's questioning. This was done differently, the council members returning to their seats while I sat beside the King. I was told not to make eye contact with him and the table had been moved so that I could not sway the King with gestures or touches.

"Provide a detailed account of your whereabouts the last day of the previous week," Council Member Warren said, his eyes watching King Sandalius. But occasionally they would flicker to me with suspicion when I moved the slightest.

"I woke and prepared for our weekly walk throughout the forest. I met with the others, speaking to Shaterria about possible messages that would be sent to the castle. We then left her and I took the lead, Rowan and Sage following behind.

I could smell that something was wrong so I continued in that direction and found the body there. Rowan and Sage took me back, and I remained in my room with Rowan for the evening."

"And what appeared to have done this to the man?" Scribbling.

"It appeared to have been done by a predator." There was a pause.

"Such as a wolf?" Warren was quick to jump on this.

"Yes, such as a wolf," the King said, pulling the words out reluctantly. He had already begun tensing, taking offense to the indirect accusation.

"And you have the ability to transform into a wolf at will. Is this correct?" Warren asked, the others watching intently. One held a pen in his hand, scribbling every word down.

"Yes." This was kept short as he was instructed; however, I could hear a hint of hostility laced within the single word. It seemed the councilmen did not notice, as they continued on without fear.

"We were informed that you left the castle several times without supervision of your guard and Rowan, who you have brought here to make you less of a beast. Is this true?" This was asked with a bit of malice, something the King caught onto.

His eyes had flickered at Warren's tone, but he did not allow it to sway him so easily. "Yes, this is true."

Council Member Warren almost seemed excited as he asked the next question. "Can you tell us what you recall from the last time you left the castle alone and when it occurred in relevance to the murder?"

The King hesitated before answering. "I last left the castle two days before I found the body. I cannot recall what happened during this time."

Warren leaned back in his chair at this, seeming to believe he was now in the lead. "If you cannot recall what happened, then tell us what you do remember. Do you remember anything odd when you gained your awareness?"

The King did not reply at first, taking a second before saying, "I was covered in blood."

Council Member Warren smirked for a brief second before changing courses. "Wolves were hunted to extinction within this forest. Who did that leave you to believe had committed this gruesome crime?"

The King's jaw clenched at the question, the silence surrounding us. "I do not know who I believed had killed him," he answered. But it was not what Council Member Warren wanted.

He raised an eyebrow before quickly saying, "You do not know? You did not question as to what could have broken a man's ribs and ripped out his tongue so viciously? Was it simply something that you were so accustomed to that you did not feel rage towards whoever had committed the crime?"

The King's posture had changed during Council Member Warren's attack. His eyes had hardened, holding the same coldness they had when I had first met him. His expression was one made of stone, portraying that he was no longer interested in talking to his guests. Even his hands, which had once been by his side, were now coiled tightly together in his lap.

"Perhaps it is time for a break," I said, my eyes turning back to the councilmen. They all turned to me, startled that I was still sitting there. They had been so involved in watching the King and waiting for an accidental confession.

"There is no time for a break. Answer the question," Warren pressed, ignoring my suggestion. I frowned but knew better than to snap at him.

I touched the King's arm, feeling it tense slightly before relaxing at the contact. However, just as I had begun calming him Warren started yelling.

"Enough, Rowan! You will be asked to leave," he snapped, pointing at my hand on the King's arm. He did not hesitate in directing his anger towards the King as well, temporarily forgetting what he was capable of.

"Who do you think did this? I will not ask again!" he exclaimed, his eyes holding a wildfire that was spreading throughout his entire body.

The King was calm as he stood up, his eyes not once leaving Council Member Warren's. He walked towards him, fear putting out the fire within seconds, and leaned until he was at eye level before saying one word: "Me." Then, he stormed out the room, the door slamming on the way out.

I followed behind him, but not before heading Warren's words. "This is not over. Your King will be found guilty and he will be killed, Rowan. Leave while you still have time."

It was not he who I ran into downstairs, but a startled looking Sage and Shaterria. Before they could question me, I asked, "Where did he go?"

"He ran outside. What happened?" Shaterria asked, her eyes filled with worry. Instead of answering, I left and was greeted by the wind. I ran towards the forest without the slightest idea of how to go about finding him.

I decided to follow the path we usually took, thinking the King would not venture somewhere else out of fear of hurting someone. It was a long walk and I was completely surrounded by nature, silence floating in the air while nature played around me. However, I did eventually find him, sitting near the rotting log that had once sheltered him from the rain.

"It was not your fault, King Sandalius. Warren was accusing you, not taking a neutral stand as he was supposed to. Do not allow him to get to you. If I did, I would not be here," I said softly before finding a spot beside him, resting my hands on the grass.

He did not reply but instead looked at me. He had calmed down, this much I could tell. His hazel eyes no longer held any sort of anger but instead held nothing. They were empty once again, simply mirroring my reflection.

"Do you truly believe you did this? Do you think you are capable of doing it?" I asked, watching as he laughed humorlessly.

"Do not forget how I earned my title, Rowan. It was by killing and nothing more," he said, his eyes flickering to a nearby tree.

I frowned before correcting myself. "You are a different person now than you were in the past. You may have been capable of doing so then, but it does not mean you would do so now."

He tilted his head, considering my words. "Am I different? I have not seen change." He was still staring at the tree with a faraway look as if thinking about something else.

I nodded at his question. "If you truly believe you have not changed, then why did you not kill Warren and the other councilmen?" To this, he did not have an answer.

We sat in silence, but within it was comfort. We remained like that, side by side, until he spoke up again, surprising me. "It is best if you leave now. I will allow you to take your father and leave without consequence. You should do so before things become worse."

He did not look at me as he said this, but at the ground. He seemed to have a resigned look as if he had accepted his fate. I was quiet before I surprised us both with my next sentence.

"I am not leaving."

He snapped his head up, hazel eyes studying me. "I have given you a free pass. You are a bigger fool than I thought if you do not take it. Do you not realize what could happen? You could potentially be blamed for it as well."

I knew this was a possibility but I would not allow it to deter me from the reason I was sent here. "Do you not remember what I told you, King Sandalius? I have told you that I do not scare easily and I still stand by those words. I will not allow you to push me away. I was sent here to help you and I am going to stay here to do just that."

I thought perhaps had annoyed him or that he would have no response because he did not speak for a few moments. I was startled when he spoke again, saying a name.

"Kieran." I blinked, confused.

"Kieran?" I repeated slowly, wondering what meaning it held.

He nodded, seeming to relax further at the name. "Yes, that is my name. I would prefer if you called me by it for the remainder of your time here," he said, a smile briefly appearing on his face.

I too smiled, momentarily forgetting about today's events. "It is a pleasure to finally meet you, Kieran."

Chapter Twenty Two

Whoop finally reached 100 pages on the word doc for this story omg. Part is just a deleted thing I decided not to use BUT it still counts. Enjoy loves! This chapter is longer than usual I definitely thought it would be short as heck.

Chapter Twenty Two

Word has spread quickly of the body of the forest, like a disease finding new victims. It had started off as being blamed by an animal but that was twisted and played with until it was now blamed on the King, who should have never left the castle.

More people began leaving, scared because of the killing. They had believed they were fine before as it had been quite some time since the King had left the castle. But now with the body, no one thought they were safe anymore.

The castle had grown so quiet that it echoed throughout each hall. I seldom saw anyone else when I walked up to the King's room, excluding the times Sage and Todd were by my side. Even the cook had left, leaving us all to fend for ourselves. Sage and I took turns cooking while Shaterria would run into town and fetch anything needed.

I had taken the King back to the castle when Sage found and informed us that the councilmen were no longer there. Since then, King Sandalius had not left his room. I supposed I would not either if I was not sure whether I killed a man or not.

I had taken to keeping him company and making sure the curtains were drawn back in an attempt to at least expose him to the sun. Todd joined me each time, although he was reluctant. But as time passed, he'd grown to learn the King was not just a predator. Now, instead of slinking into a corner, he would sniff around the room in curiosity before finding something to mess with.

At the moment, I was with the King who was sitting in a chair with his head in his hands. I could see his thumbs rubbing his temples in a slow, circular motion as if trying to smooth out his irritations. However, it did not seem to be working because he'd been doing so for quite some time.

"Kieran," I murmured, hoping to catch his attention. I came upstairs every day in hopes of continuing the conditioning we'd been working on. I would talk to him and get him to walk around the room, sometimes guiding him downstairs when I assured him that most had already left. He would believe me occasionally, but for most days he did not, just as he hadn't today.

It had succeeded, his hazel eyes flickering up and studying mine. "Perhaps a walk will help? We do not have to stray far," I said, watching as he shook his head immediately.

Sage, who had been keeping Todd company, spoke up. "We can all walk downstairs. We do not have to leave the walls of the castle. Most have packed and left so we will most likely not encounter another." I looked at him briefly, giving him a thankful gaze, before walking closer to the King.

"I am not going downstairs. That is final," he said firmly, looking away from me and out the window. No matter how hard he worked, I could catch a glimpse of longing in his eyes. He'd experienced the outside world for the first time in a long time and had just begun to realize what he had been missing.

"You cannot continue to sit here moping like a child!" I snapped, both pairs of eyes turning towards me. I frowned, crossing my arms. "I will stand by what I said. I allowed you to take it easy for a bit because I knew this was hard but you cannot progress if you do not go anywhere but in this room. There's only so much we can do here," I said a little more softly, my voice losing the edge it had.

The King was improving, that much I could say with unwavering certainty. However, he was already beginning to retreat back into the man I had met before, losing his hope and any bit of change that had happened. Staying in this room would only continue his downward spiral until he crashed at the bottom.

Sage appeared a bit annoyed at my snapped, but that was something I had gotten used to. Kieran was his King and he was not fond of seeing another talk to him in any other manner than respect. So I simply shot him a look back before focusing on the King once again.

"Perhaps Sage can lead the way and scout for anyone. You will have a warning if we approach someone," I suggested, watching as he began rubbing his temples again.

I frowned. He was not paying the slightest attention to my idea. I walked towards him, grabbing his hands with my own and pulling them from his head. His eyes jumped towards mine, startled by the sudden interaction.

"If you do not try then we are going nowhere. I would be helping equally if I just left. Do you not understand this?" He continued watching me for a moment, neither one of us saying anything. It was not until Todd began scratching at the floor, breaking the silence, that he spoke again.

"We will go downstairs but only for a brief moment. I have no desire to spend more time than necessary." He was still looking at me, his stare unyielding. I nodded in reply before letting go of his hands and straightening up.

Sage was already walking towards the door, waiting by it. The King stood up and we walked towards Sage together. The second Sage opened the door, Todd ran out and towards the end of the hall, chattering excitedly to himself. He was not enjoying spending all of his time indoors, no matter how large the castle was.

We all left, going out of the hall and down the stairs. We then began walking, Todd having darted far ahead of us and disappearing. Sage was ahead as well but within view.

"When I was younger, it was impossible to walk within the castle without spotting another. However, now it seems to have completely reserves itself," the King said softly, looking at the empty halls and rooms surrounding him.

I was quiet, wondering whether he missed his past. Did he regret killing the man who had brought him here, the former King who had treated him as his own child? Or perhaps the man never crossed his mind.

As if reading my mind, he spoke again. "I prefer it this way. I used to walk throughout these halls and eyes would follow me no matter the occasion. I wore the same skin as them, yet they seemed to see me in a different light than they saw themselves." I frowned while nodding, understanding this too well.

"It is as if you are silently being shunned out. It is worse in a way than if they had simply voiced their opinions," I replied, gazing in front of us. I could hear him make a low sound, one of agreement.

"Do you miss the King and Queen?" I asked, hearing him scoff in reply.

"Behind closed doors, they did not act the same as they did when we were all in public," he started while we turned a corner heading closer towards the kitchen.

"They would smile and way when their staff and people were nearby, but when it was just us, they were strict. It was not easy for me to adjust to this new lifestyle but they did not care.

They were ruthless and punished me each time I failed to compress my natural instincts. They would tell me I was too animalistic and that they would throw me back out if I did not straighten up. By this time, the wolves were gone and I would have nowhere to return to. Despite what seems to be popular opinion, the witch helped me when she turned me into this."

I did not respond, unsure of how to do so. The former King had not been as kind and generous towards Keiran as he was portrayed, nor had Keiran been happy with them. He had been taken from the forest and brought into a place that walked around him with caution while I had been pushed from such a place into a forest that accepted me. Both were so different yet shared more similarities that I had noticed.

By the time we reached the kitchen, I could hear the castle doors yawning open. I walked away from the King and towards the front in time to see Shaterria coming in with bags while Todd darted outside.

"Todd!" I snapped, running outside. By the time I got there, he was nowhere to be seen. My lips turned down, my heart beating irregularly. He could be anywhere and so could the person who had killed the man.

"He will be fine. He can handle himself."

I turned, seeing Sage beside me, having run after me. I huffed, disagreeing but I knew his words were true in a sense. Although my little one was not capable of fending off a predator, he would know better than to trust a stranger.

"There is a reason Todd lives with me and not in the forest," I replied, glancing around once more before heading inside. I would go out and check for him in a bit.

We both headed for the kitchen, where we found the King helping Shaterria unload the bags of supplies for today's meal. It was my turn to cook and we had decided on steak, baked potatoes, and a fresh salad.

Once Shaterria and the King finished unloading everything, Shaterria turned towards me. "Perhaps we can all help you today. I have finished my errands and it does not seem as if you all were doing anything of importance. It will get done faster, yes?" she suggested, looking at the others.

"Have you ever cooked?" I asked, looking towards the King. He would be as useless as Todd in the kitchen.

He shook his head before finding a stool to sit on. "I will not be assisting as I do not think I will be much help. But I will watch," he said but it was my turn to disagree.

"You can help me with the salad. I will tell you what to do. Sage and Shaterria can do the rest," I said, looking at the others who nodded. The King stood up again and followed me, watching as I gathered the ingredients we would be needing.

"Grab two knives and a large bowl. It will make cutting the vegetables go faster," I instructed, bringing the ingredients with me and setting them on the counter. I could feel his presence nearby as I pulled out the tomatoes, handing them to him.

"You will cut these while I peel and slice the cucumbers," I said, looking at him for confirmation. He nodded, grabbing the tomatoes from me while I grabbed the other knife.

I could hear Shaterria and Sage talking lightly about nothing in particular while she baked the potatoes and he seared the steaks. I was peeling the second cucumber when I glanced over towards the King, pausing in my action.

"Have you ever seen your tomato cut like that in a salad?" I asked him, laughing despite the mess he had made. He had sliced the tomato into thick pieces meant for a hamburger if anything. Even that was messy as if he'd squeezed the tomato too hard and he had not cut off the top or bottom.

"Did I not tell you I have not cooked?" he replied back, but instead of harsh, his voice held a light tone to it. I smiled, taking the other tomato.

"Just cut those in half and we will make do with them. I will cut this one and perhaps you can do the last one correctly." I said, setting the tomato sideways before quickly cutting off both ends then flipping it back over.

I could feel the King's intense stare on me as I cut the tomato in half, cutting each half into another half again and again until they were bite size. I finished, placing them in the bowl and glancing up at the King.

"Are you capable of doing that much or can the precious royalty not handle a tomato?" I asked with an arched eyebrow, crossing my arms. I watched as his eyes sparked, a shine forming in them.

"And if I am, what do I receive in return? I believe when an animal is trained, you reward it, do you not?" he asked, causing me to nod. I fed those who ventured towards me in the forest, rewarding them for trusting me.

"What would you like? Perhaps do not aim too high. I do not have a lot of faith as it seems you squeezed the life out of the last one," I said, glancing at the all the tomato's juices on the counter.

"A night with you."

I blinked, anger rising at my first thought. "I am not-" I started, my voice growing with each word but he was quick to interrupt me, laughing.

"Do not think so crudely, Rowan. I simply meant spending time with you during the night, nothing more. I do not sleep well and would enjoy the company," he explained, causing me to blush. However, I did not look away, refusing to give him the satisfaction.

"Fine. Cut the last two tomatoes and Sage and I-"

He shook his head. "No, Sage will not be joining us. It will only be the two of us as he will not be needed. I will not pull him from his sleep too."

I hesitated, thinking about the first time I had met the King. Had it not been for Sage pulling me back, I would have been a victim of his anger, which had been caused by my own temper. They both did not work well together and the only buffer we had was Sage. Without Sage, there was no telling what would happen.

"If you can cut these two tomatoes perfectly I will agree to spend the night with you," I said after a minute. I then watched in amazement as he cut both tomatoes without hesitation.

I narrowed my eyes while he placed them in the bowl. "Did you lie? Have you cut them before?" I pressed, refusing to believe it was his first time anymore.

He smiled, shaking his head. "I am a quick learner. Did you truly believe I would not be able to cut a tomato? It was not a difficult task," he replied and I ignored him, handing him the head of lettuce.

"Tear this and put it in the bowl," I said, hearing his laughter after. "What?" I asked, annoyed.

"Are you competitive? Are you not able to accept the fact that I did as you asked?" I could tell from his tone that he was enjoying this, the fact that he had succeeded my expectations.

I frowned, throwing the cucumber slices into the bowl before moving on to the onion. Before I could peel off the first layer, I felt a hand brush along my cheek and causing me to drop my knife.

"Are you mad at me?" His tone had changed from light to now sounding confused. He had leaned closer, his face level with my own. I was startled, tempting to flee, but my back was already against the counter. His hazel eyes stared at me, searching for any clue.

"No," I replied shortly, at a loss for words. He watched me a moment longer as if attempting to check if I was telling the truth or not. "I am fine, Keiran. I am not mad," I added once I found my voice again. "Go back to tearing your lettuce. That is something you are decent at."

His expression changed back, clear or the confusion. I could hear him laugh before he went back to tearing the lettuce. I continued cutting the onion, thinking about how different he was. Even his personality had changed. He was no longer harsh and quick to anger. Yet, even just now, he still held the beautiful, mysterious aura of a wolf.

Chapter Twenty Three

TWO IMPORTANT THINGS: Hello! I have completely outlined this story and it is going to be AROUND a total of 35 chapters so we are getting pretty close to the ending, unfortunately. ANOTHER exciting thing: I made a book on my profile where you can post summaries of your story if you'd like me to read it! I truly hope you'll check it out because I'm interested in getting to see y'all's stories and works. The book is called "Sharing is Caring"

Chapter Twenty Three

Our dinner was quiet for the most part, Sage and Shaterria the only two attempting to converse. The King did not say a word while I would occasionally speak when something was directed towards me. However, it was not awkward but soothing to me.

I was now preparing for my night with the King, as promised. My hair was braided down for the night while I wore clothes suitable for the night. I found myself standing in front of the door leading to the King's door, hesitating before knocking.

There was silence before I briefly heard him say, "Come in." I opened the door, walking in and spotting him standing by his table, running a finger along it. As usual, he didn't bother with looking up once I entered.

"I have a request if I am to go through with this," I said, standing by the door, not having yet closed it. I watched as he finally looked at me, curiosity in his eyes as he tilted his head.

"You lost a bet, Rowan. You are in no position to make requests," he said but kept his eyes on me. I took this as a positive sign, conveying that he was not yet dismissing me.

I crossed my arms across my chest before saying, "I will keep you company if we spend a bit of it outside. I have-"

"No." This was followed by a frown before his eyes finally looked away, briefly skittering towards the window then the wall.

I pursed my lips together, attempting to keep from grinding my teeth. "I have to look for Todd! I will stay the night as long as I can-"

He interrupted yet again, his voice holding more frustration than before. "I have no interest in roaming outside. We are going to spend the night inside. That is final."

I clicked my tongue, looking up at the ceiling to keep from losing my patience. "You expect me to spend the night while my little one is out there? He could potentially run into someone who's willing to cause him harm. I cannot stay here and do that," I snapped, watching as his eyes flashed before he closed them.

There was a pause before he finally spoke. "I am no negotiating with a woman who does not know where her boundaries lie. You agreed to spend the night and we are not going outside. Is that too difficult for you to comprehend?" he asked, his eyes holding a small fire. My own narrowed, refusing to give in.

"I will not feel the least bit guilty for choosing Todd over a man who does not know when to give in to his childish arrogance. Is that too difficult for you to comprehend?" I asked back.

Without waiting for his response I went out the door, walking down the hall. We were both getting nowhere with each other and I did not intend to go without checking for Todd. I had foolishly attempted to reason with a man who did not know what the word meant.

King Sandalius moved in a similar fashion that a wolf did. Both creatures were silent in their footsteps, quiet enough that their prey was oblivious to their presence. I had not expected to be deaf to his footsteps, nor had I expected him to follow me.

I was surprised when a hand grabbed my forearm, whirling me around. I stumbled, falling against the King. As I attempted to pull away, he pressed his arm against my back, limiting my movement.

He was shaking ever so slightly and I could feel his chest rising and falling unsteadily. I pulled back enough to see his face where I could spot sweat forming along his hairline. His eyes had begun to change as well, the hazel color more pronounced than ever. I was not sure what was occurring, but something was happening.

"Keiran?" I asked, my anger momentarily forgotten. His eyes flickered down to me, staring for a moment before he seemed to register that I was speaking to him.

"You cannot go. You cannot break your promise to a King. That solely is reasoning for punishment, Rowan," he said, but even his voice shook at his own words.

I frowned, taking advantage of his momentary unstable condition, shoving away from him. He staggered backward, managing to catch himself before his eyes flared, his anger spreading and making his body more steady.

"Then punish me. I will see you tomorrow since you are beyond reason. Goodnight," I said stiffly, turning to walk away once again. I was at the end of the hall, opening the door when I could hear the grunting of a man and the tearing of clothes.

I paused, turning to spot the King. He was no longer human, but a large black-furred wolf. I watched as he lowered his head, a growl building in his throat. I continued watching, considering my odds. I could make it down the hall by closing the door on him, however, Sage had informed me that the only door that held the King in was the door to his room. They had yet to replace the ones in the halls so it was possible that with enough time, he would break the doors. Yet, it was my only option.

I took my opportunity, running out of the hall and slamming the door shut. I could hear him barrel into the door, its frame already giving way while he snarled in fury. I ran down the steps, opening the last door before closing it. I then found a room near my own to hide in, deciding it was safer than going outdoors.

It wasn't much longer before I could hear the front door being slammed open and then a howl, signaling the King's exit. I frowned, mentally cursing myself. He was outside, the very place he needs to avoid while he was a wolf. If someone saw him, they were not likely to take it well and report it to the councilmen who'd forbidden him from shifting outside. If the found out, he'd be dragged out and killed.

I paced the room for a while, allowing my thoughts to run around before they settled and I decided the best thing was to find the King. I did not want to be the one responsible for his death, even if his own arrogance had led to it. While I was searching for him, I could also search for my little one at the same time.

I went to my room, grabbing a jacket and well as appropriate shoes. It was cool, a gentle breeze riding through the air. Night had fallen long ago, crickets chirping their seasonal song. There was no lighting outside, my familiarity with the forest being my only guide throughout it.

"Keiran," I said softly, calling his name over and over. There was a chance that exhaustion had taken ahold of him and he'd already shifted back. I was holding on to that and hoping that he would hear me before giving me a signal that he was nearby.

However, that is not what happened. I spent hours searching, each one ticking by while my frustration grew. I could not spot any sign of King Sandalius or Todd. They both seemed to have disappeared, leaving no trace behind.

I found myself leaning against a tree, folding my hands behind my head while I looked up at the sky. The stars were out, twinkling and greeting me cheerily. Yet, I could not find the strength to return their energy. This night had gone downhill very quickly and showed no signs of slowing down anytime soon.

It was then that it began to rain, the breeze blowing the droplets underneath the tree and towards me. I blew out air, hugging myself but it was useless. Within minutes my clothes were wet and it was not soon before I would become drenched in water.

I began searching the forest again, retracing my steps. The temperature had dropped dramatically, as the coldness was no longer friendly but harsh and unrelenting. Just as I considered searching for Sage and asking him for help, I froze spotting a wolf.

He was standing in front of me, his fur completely soaked. His eyes were unblinking as he watched me shivering, looking at him. I walked towards him slowly, stopping when his muscles bunched up.

"I mean no harm," I said gently. I held out my hand, waiting patiently. We were like that for a while before he cautiously inched forward, his snout stretching out and sniffing my hand. His eyes seemed to register something familiar about my scent because he stepped forward, stopping when he was right in front of me.

I ran my hands through his fur, pushing the water out. When my hand reached his face, he leaned into it, his eyes closing. "You remind me of my little one," I said softly, a smile finding its way onto my face. I ran my fingers along his ears and neck, making sure to scratch both areas.

I pulled my hand away but before I could stand, he pressed his muzzle into my hand. I laughed lightly, speaking to him. "You're as docile as Todd, yet-"

My words turned into silence as I drew back my hand, covered in a liquid thicker than water. Even in the darkness, I could see the tainted red color and smell its sharp scent. I glanced at the King, only now noticing the hairs on his muzzle were matted together in different spots, saturated in blood.

I could feel a sense of dread settling in the back of my mind, screaming louder and louder. My heart stopped its pacing, freezing with time. Just like that, the King was forgotten as I stood up and began searching around us, looking.

When I finally found him, he was underneath a bush, curled up on himself. His eyes were closed and his fur soaked by a crude mixture of rain and blood. My vision was blurred by tears as I spotted the gaping wound, my emotions running wild. I could not tell whether he was breathing or not and knew even if he was, he was likely to not make it.

"Todd."

Chapter Twenty Four

A little short but I still hope you all enjoy! This chapter is dedicated to the beautiful Holland_Italy for her moodboard that is shown above I think? This one is Rowan's and the nex chapter will feature the King's!

Chapter Twenty Four

Sage and Shaterria were waiting for me when I arrived, Sage's facial expression turning grim when his eyes landed on the bloody bundle of fur in my arms. They were both silent, neither having a sarcastic remark.

"I will search for the King. Assist Rowan," Shaterria said quietly and for once, Sage did not argue. As I entered, Shaterria rushed in, grabbing a coat and shoes before going outside in the rain.

I walked into my own room, gently placing Todd onto the bed before silently grabbing the first aid kit. Sage walked in shortly after, coming to my side. "How can I help?" he asked, his voice without anger or annoyance.

"Grab a rag. We need to clean the area," I said, Sage leaving right after and coming back quickly.

Neither one of us spoke as we worked together, the silence surrounding us like a blanket. I found myself whispering to my little one, telling him to hold on for just a little longer and that all would be fine. I had saved him once and would do so again.

We finished doing all we could and I left Todd on the bed, running my hand along him as Sage cleaned up. "All will be fine, my little one," I whispered to him, leaning down to press my lips to his head. I stayed like that for a moment, my eyes closed, before Sage joined my side once again.

"The King has been found and is in his room. Shaterria investigated the area and found scraps nearby," Sage said softly and I shook my head. Of course. The only way Todd was to trust a stranger was through the offering of food, his greatest weakness.

I stood, look at the wall as I finally spoke. "I will be leaving. Todd and I will pick up my father-"

"Rowan," Sage tried, his voice holding caution.

My eyes turned towards him, holding a burning fire. "No, Sage. This-" I hissed, pointing at Todd who was oblivious to the world around us. "-is not what we agreed to. I could handle myself and handle if someone's wrath was directed towards me. But what I will not do is stand by while they hurt one of the two that I hold closest." Sage was quiet, considering my words.

"I understand-" Once again, I was quick to cut him off, his word choice angering me.

"No, you do not! Your King is fine as is Shaterria. They have not been harmed in the slightest. But Todd has and is going to die because of this place!" I snapped, pausing to calm myself before adding, "I am sorry but I am not willing to sacrifice him for King Sandalius' well-being."

It was his turn to glare at me, a frown falling upon his face. "Do you think I do not know the pain of losing those closest to you? Think for once, Rowan, instead of speaking impulsively. I was here before all fled. I had friends and family. Do you think it was easy for me to watch them pack and leave, to claim I was foolish for standing by the side of a man who would eventually kill me? It was not, yet I am still here." For that, I had nothing to say, my anger dying down.

We both fell quiet and I watched as his own anger ceased. He ran a hand through his hair, sighing, before speaking again. "Perhaps the best place for your father and Todd would be at home if you truly worry for them. It is far away from here and familiar to your fox. Your father's servant will be sent with him, along with whatever he needs. Will this suffice?' he asked, awaiting my answer.

I turned, my eyes falling on my little one. It would be better for him at home, regardless of whether I was there or not. Todd did not put up with my father, but if he was all that was left, my little one would sacrifice his ways for his needs. However, my father was happy here.

I did not want to ruin his happiness with others, here in a town. He was able to live normally and did not have to keep to himself. He could go out as he pleased without being hassled. But I knew this would have to end eventually and we would all find our way back home.

If Todd and my father returned home without me and I stayed, perhaps I could renegotiate with the King and Sage. I would ask for my father to have a permanent place within the town, where he could live happily. It would be hard, but I would return home by myself after all of this and visit him often.

"A place for my father when this is over. I desire a home within the town for him, for free. I will stay if this is given," I said quietly, exhausted. It had been a long day and I had a feeling it would not end anytime soon.

"I will have that arranged," Sage replied, his voice holding a relieved note. "I know this is not easy but I appreciate your help, Rowan. Thank you," he said, walking closer to me.

"Todd will be fine as well. I have not seen any animal handle hardships as well as yours," he added, bringing a small smile to my face. Sage was right. Todd was stronger than any animal - than any person - I knew of.

"Of course he will. Isn't that right, my little one?" I said softly, reaching down to pet him again. I watched as Sage joined, running his own hand along Todd as well. I laughed quietly, thinking about how he would've cherished the amount of attention he was receiving right now if he could.

It was not long before Sage and I heard the castle's door open with an explosive boom, signaling that our day was, in fact, not yet over.

Chapter Twenty Five

I apologize for the shortness but I hope y'all still enjoy! I'll be going back and dedicating chapter to readers!

Chapter Twenty Five

"Did you contact them?"

I glanced at Sage, narrowing my eyes. "I thought you were one to use your common sense. When would I have had time to contact the councilmen between patching Todd up, hmm?" I snapped, Sage glaring before we both turned our attention back to the current situation.

Council member Warren stood to the side with a smug smirk on his face while guards were escorting King Sandalius outside. His feet and arms had been restrained by chains while there was also one around his neck. We asked if this was necessary only to be told that when dealing with a beast you treat them as such.

The King did not resist but allowed them to treat him as if he was a beast. Shaterria stood to the side watching as well, her face holding an angered look. She knew just as well as we did that nothing could be done.

"What new evidence was provided that allowed you to take him?" I asked, Council member Warren turning his attention to me with a grimace. But it was quick to turn into a coy smile.

"We weren't given new evidence. You see, Rowan, your King turned himself in," he explained, surprising Sage and I. Shaterria, however, still held the same expression as if this was not news to her.

I turned towards her, snapping, "Did you have something to do with this?" Her face turned to stone at the accusation, looking towards Sage for help. But he stood by me, waiting for an answer as well.

"I do as the King says, unlike you. He told me it was time and to send for the councilmen. I attempted to reason with him but he had no interest in changing his decision," she snapped back, piercing eyes staring me down.

I bit back a reply, looking towards Warren who appeared pleased with himself. "This is not over," I said firmly but he just shook his head.

"Ah, but it is, isn't it? Who are you here to tame now? Your job is gone, Rowan. Now you can pack up and leave. Isn't that what you wanted all along?" he asked, smirking when he received no reply.

All of us followed as he walked out, telling them to load the King into the cart. I clicked my tongue in irritation, upset with the conditions of the transportation. It looked like a vehicle made for catching stray animals on the street before they were euthanized.

I could see the King's hazel eyes watching us from inside, as mysterious as always. I did not see fear, worry, or concern about his own fate. It seemed like he had accepted his fate and would make no move to change it.

"Let's go!" Council member Warren snapped, the horses running off not at the sound of his words, but at the whip biting into their skin. We all watched until the disappeared down the road, no one else in sight.

"Your wish has now been granted. Congratulations." I whirled around at Sage's harsh words in time to see him walking away. Shaterria looked between the two of us before deciding it was better to stay out of it, walking in the opposite direction. I huffed, walking after Sage.

"Excuse me?" I snapped, loud enough I was sure he had heard me. Yet, he continued on as if I had not spoken, walking without hesitation in his steps.

"I know you heard me!" I yelled, walking a little faster, grabbing his arm. He whirled around, a storm lurking in his eyes. He was upset with the events that had just unfolded, yet I was not to blame. I did not tell the King to call for the councilmen. That was a decision he had come to on his own.

"If you had not ventured outside, this would not have happened. The King would not have called the councilmen out of guilt for something he did not do," he said lowly, containing his anger for the time being.

I scoffed before replying bitterly. "Is he all that matters to you, your precious King? If I did not go outside, Todd would have been dead! I have no regrets and would do so again, understand that." Sage narrowed his eyes before he laughed humorlessly at my words.

"You are not much different, Rowan. You care only for yourself and two others. Do not accuse me of callousness when you are the same way," he paused before his lips turned down and he added, "You have been granted your wish. You wanted an opportunity to leave and now you have one." With that, he walked away, leaving me alone.

He was right. I had no responsibility to stay here anymore. The King was no longer here, so I did not have a job. So I packed my things, making a crude shift to carry Todd in, and left.

Chapter Twenty Six

- -

S orry for the wait, my loves! It wasn't because I'm on hiatus again but I struggled with a part in this chapter sksk. But today I got through it so I hope y'all enjoy!

Chapter Twenty Six

I was leaning against the doorway, watching as Todd scratched at the front door before turning towards me, cocking his head. I laughed softly, walking over to him.

"Not yet, little one." I kneeled down, running my hands through his fur. He chattered back, tilting his head in confusion. I reached into my pocket, pulling out of a piece of meat. "Soon you will be well enough to go back into our forest, do not worry." He became distracted by the meat, snatching it up quickly before running off.

"Rowan, sweetheart, I think I have to go into town. It seems we're out of a few things," my father said from within the kitchen as the cabinet's doors yawned open and slammed shut. I sighed, knowing he was right.

We'd been away from home for quite some time. However, I knew it was always tasking on my father to go get them. It would likely be harder now that he was out of the routine of doing so.

I hesitated before responding. "Do not worry, Papa. I will go into town and buy what we need." I could hear silence in the kitchen before I saw him walking into the living room, a frown on his face.

"You certainly won't be doing that. You and I both know they don't accept you and won't sell you anything. I'll go." I shook my head, already grabbing my shoes and putting them on.

He walked closer, quickly taking my jacket before I had the chance to grab it. I gave him a pointed look before speaking. "It is not like you to play childish games," I teased, but it did nothing to lessen the expression on his face.

"You are not going out." He said the words firmly, little room for compromising. I took his hands in mine tightly, pressing my lips against them.

"Papa, I will be fine. I will go to the town I have gone to during emergencies. It will be easier now that we have a horse once again," I explained, hoping he would see my reasoning. "You are not fit to continue going back and forth to town. I will go from now on. Just make sure Todd does not go out."

I gently pulled my jacket from his hands, grateful he allowed me to do so. I could see the reluctance in his face, how badly he wanted to find an excuse for me to not go. But we both knew it was the best solution and we could not go argue about it.

"Be safe, sweetheart. Don't stray from the path. Come back right after, do you hear me?" he asked sternly, lecturing me as if I was a little girl.

I smiled, grabbing the money from him before giving him a hug. "I will be fine, Papa. Hopefully, Todd does not cause you too much trouble. If he becomes too restless, there are toys in the cardboard box within my room." We both said parting words before I left.

In order to return home, I'd asked Shaterria if I could borrow a horse. She had told me yes before telling me not to worry about returning this particular one. She explained that it had once belonged to a knight who had died, sacrificing his life for the King. They had kept the horse in hopes of finding another life for him. Shaterria said that he would be serving an equally important purpose if he was placed into my care. I thanked her, promising I would take great care of him.

I got him ready for the ride before smiling, running my hand down his mane. "I hope you are enjoying your time here. Are you ready for a ride?" I asked him, hearing air rush out of his nose in response. I took that as a yes before I mounted him, beginning our journey.

It was a long ride but I did not complain. It was either this or have my father ride into the closest town when it would only bring down his health. At least the weather was in a kind mood, the sun wearing a gown made of white clouds, her light shining so bright that it filtered through on occasion.

When we finally arrived in the town, the staring had begun. I could as they tried to steal not-so-discreet glances towards me, their stares boring into my back. I ignored them, continuing towards the center of the town where the needed supplies would be.

"Isn't that the woman who drives animals crazy? I heard she does it with a snap of her fingers."

"No, no. She just stares at them. I think she can communicate with them telepathically. Say the wrong thing and she'll tell that horse to charge at us without speaking a word."

"Maybe she can't actually do it. She couldn't be bothered to tame the King, after all."

I willed myself to stop listening, knowing the comments would build and build until someone decided that I had convinced the King to kill the man. It was the worst possible scenario and likely in all of their eyes.

I dismounted Deuis, the horse I'd been gifted, before making sure he was placed in the nearby visiting stable. I then headed into the local store, noticing when the talking turned into muted whispers.

I walked down the aisles, holding my head high, refusing to allow the stares of simple-minded people to weigh me down. However, their stares seemed to have a magical effect capable of causing time to warp, seconds feeling as long as minutes, minutes as long as hours. By the time I grabbed all of my necessities, it felt as if I had been inside the store for a lifetime.

I placed my things on the counter, ignoring the cold look I received from the clerk. I believed if I acted as if nothing was out of the ordinary, they would continue whispering and leave me be. I was proven wrong when the clerk grabbed my things and instead of placing them in bags, placed them in the nearby trash.

My eyes flickered with surprise before they glazed over, hardening into orbs of invincible glass. My spine seemed to become a cord of steel as I straightened up, my hands clenching and unclenching quickly. I would not allow someone so petty to get to me.

"Is there a problem?" I asked calmly, however, just my voice alone caused the people nearby to quiet, turning their attention towards us.

He crossed his arms, shifting his feet. It was clear by his stance that he was portraying someone who was not threatened. Yet, his eyes were what gave him away, as they did most people's true emotions. They were as wide as a newborn deer's.

"I want nothing to do with you or your business. No one would've bought those things after hearing you were the one who held them previously," he said stiffly, his eyes staring me down. I gritted my teeth, hoping my temper would not get the best of me, especially in front of an expectant crowd.

"I am bringing you business. I am willing to pay more if that is what it takes-" I started but he quickly shook his head, silently cutting me off.

"You're going to destroy my business! Don't you understand? The second they hear that you showed up here they'll be looking towards my competitor's store," he snapped, growing angrier by the second. I could feel the tension thickening, eagerly watching the tense conversation.

"Fine," I growled, storming out of the store. Making a scene would do me no good. It would only provide fuel to the burning fire. As it was, I was already doing so by coming into the town.

I expected to ride back home and tell my father that we would order the supplies. They would come much later but it was the only solution. I knew he would fight me on this but I would not allow him to ride into town anymore. But, before I could start listing the benefits of having the supplies sent to the house, I spotted a familiar mare.

"Hello, Sequeria. It seems that you are doing well," I said softly to her, my body relaxing as I ran a hand over her, hearing her quietly nicker in response. I pressed my forehead to hers, her tranquil nature rushing through my body, providing me with a sense of calmness.

"Do you think it is appropriate to interact with someone else's horse without their permission?"

I frowned, the calmness leaving my body as I turned, meeting a pair of light brown eyes. He wore a plain white shirt and jeans, his hair pulled back into a ponytail. Within his hands were bags that he thrust towards me when he was within reach. I scowled but grabbed them on reflex.

"I am not your servant. Take your bags before I drop them on the ground," I said, watching as his eyes rolled, already growing impatient with me.

"They are yours. I visited your home and your father told me that you had gone into this town to buy supplies. I bought a variety of common things that most need. I assume you have not yet gotten them?" he questioned, raising his eyebrow. I was silent for once, shaking my head. He did not need to know that I had tried getting supplies only to fail miserably. I glanced in the bags, noting there were a few things we still needed but they were not things that we needed now.

He nodded in reply before gently petting Sequeria then mounting her. "I will meet you back at your house. We have much to discuss." This was all he said before he rode off, leaving my irritated and beyond frustrated.

By the time Deuis and I returned, Sequeria was eating some food that had been provided. I tied Deuis up next to her, murmuring goodbyes to the both of them before I took my supplies and walked into the house.

It was quite odd, seeing Sage in this setting. Perhaps I would find it odd if anyone was inside other than my father and Todd, as we didn't have guests. But what was most startling was how he seemed to blend in with the surroundings like it was the most natural thing.

My father sat on the couch, Sage on the adjacent one. The two were conversing with one another, each smiling occasionally. Todd had been curled on Sage's lap grooming himself before he spotted me and began chattering excitedly, walking towards me.

"I've missed you too, little one," I said, smiling as I picked him up, walking over and sitting next to my father. "Would you mind making hot chocolate, Papa?" I asked, knowing it was best if Sage and I conversed alone.

He grinned before clapping his hands. "That sounds wonderful, sweetheart. I'll go do just that!" he exclaimed, pressing a kiss to my cheek before he got up and disappeared into the kitchen.

"We found a slaughtered wolf within the forest. Someone attempted to feed bits to Todd," Sage abruptly said, not bothering with small talk. I suppose it was for the best because I was not one for beating around the bush either.

I was quietly, petting Todd as I considered my words. "That does not concern me anymore, Sage. My job ended the moment the King was taken away. It is why I am home and you know this."

His jaw hardened at my words, but he surprised me when he didn't snap back, but instead spoke with a leveled tone. "This is evidence of the King's innocence, Rowan. He would never kill his own kind. He was a wolf when Todd was injured as well so he could not have tried feeding him." He paused for a moment before speaking again. "I am here because I need your help."

I pursed my lips, thinking of the last time he had asked for the same thing. It had ended with Todd almost dead and me failing to do the job I was given. My father had been better off, however, he'd grown accustomed to a higher standard of living as had I. Living here again would not be easy.

"I can provide your father with reliable housing once again. Todd can remain with him or wherever you would prefer."

There was silence again before I decided to reply. "This is not about where they will stay, Sage. This is about their safety. Even so, I do not believe there is hope when there are so many factors going against the King. I understand that you are loyal to him but reason states that this will not end well for him whether I am here or within the castle."

Sage's eyes flashed before his face became empty. But not quick enough. I could spot the disappointment that had lingered behind, causing me to look away.

"I did not believe you were one to give up." With that, he got up, said goodbye to my father and left.

Chapter Twenty Seven

C hapter Twenty Seven

"Are you sure you are going to be okay?" It was different, leaving him alone out here in the forest.

He just waved a dismissive hand in my direction, practically shoving me out the door with a smile. "Sweetheart, I'm not going to wither away without you. Lily agreed to come down in a few days and help me. I can be on my own until then. Now go," he urged and I sighed, turning to hug him tightly.

"Todd and I will be back soon enough, I promise. Make sure not to do anything too tasking-" I tried, but he shook his head pulling away from me and laughing. I had thought about leaving Todd behind but knew he would not behave with my father. So I would keep him closeby at all times.

"Rowan, I don't need you lecturing me. Go now before you manage to convince yourself you need to stay." He was right. That was exactly what I was doing in my mind, conjuring up the worst possible scenarios.

"I love you, Papa," I said with a brief smile. He watched as Deuis, Todd and I all left, galloping towards the castle.

The ride there was as long and tedious as I had remembered. We did not stop to rest often, only doing so when I noticed Deuis was becoming tired or needed to eat. I would eat as well, making sure to feed Todd and tell him we would be there soon.

When we finally arrived, the three of us were exhausted by the travelling. Deuis had begun walking at a slower pace, perking up a bit when he recognized the castle. Even Todd, who'd chattered non-stop in my ear the entire time, had gone quiet some time ago and just slept.

It was quiet when we stopped and I dismounted Deuis, murmuring thankful words to him. The silence was not a peaceful one, but one that slithered through right before Death took his opportunity to wreak havoc.

When I placed Deuis within the stable, I noticed that there was only a single horse left. All the other stalls had been cleaned and emptied, causing me to wonder if I was too late. I put Deuis into the stall next to Sequeria, brushing him before making sure they both had adequate supplies and leaving with Todd.

I walked into the castle, tensing as the sounds of my footsteps echoed throughout the building, bouncing from wall to wall. Despite how loud they seemed, I was the only one who was there to hear them.

It had been quite empty before my departure but this was different. There used to be servants who would walk through every now and again or perhaps there would be a guard on his way to the front of the castle. Now, I was not sure that I was not alone in the castle.

I walked through, knowing where I would find him if he was here. He would have either been tending to his horse or within his own room. The latter was where I found him, placing clothes into a suitcase and other small items into a bag.

I knew he had heard me open the door. He knew it was me that stood there waiting, however, he continued packing, not once glancing in my direction. I bit down the snarky comment that desired to be said, knowing it would not help.

"Where are you going?" I asked, deciding it was the safest route to travel on. He still kept his eyes on his suitcase, quiet. I thought perhaps he would not answer but he finally spoke after a moment.

"There is no one to take the throne so the castle is going to be torn down. We were all told to leave beforehand." I frowned, glancing at my feet. It seemed I was too late. Yet, I didn't leave.

"And when the King returns how am I to tell him that his most loyal guard ran off?" I asked with a raised eyebrow. His eyes finally met mine, but only for a second before they drifted away.

"I am not interested in your help anymore, Rowan. You wished to go home and that is exactly where you should be now."

I gritted my teeth at his response, my patience dwindling quickly. "Stop acting like a child and forgive me, Sage! I may not have responded at first but I am here now." I stepped closer to him, placing my hand on his, stopping its movement. "Is it not better late than never?" I asked, grabbing his chin and forcing him to look at me.

His eyes were expressionless at first, however, they finally softened after a second and he briefly nodded. I was surprised when his arms wrapped around my waist, encasing me while my body was pressed against his own. I could feel his hair tickling my nose and the softness of his skin on my cheek causing my heart to race.

"Thank you for coming, Rowan. I know this does not mean much to you-" I clicked my tongue at his words, startling him into silence as I pulled away slightly, his arms loosely around me.

"Sage, I may pretend that I do not care for you or the King but I think the both of you have grown on me. I may not care for the King as much as you but I do care. I promised that I would help tame the King and I cannot do that if he is gone," I explained, his expression turning tender at my words.

I could see his eyes flicker as the silence returned, holding something that I could not identify quick enough. However, it left when Todd finally decided to poke out his head, chattering animatedly when he noticed Sage.

Sage laughed at Todd's antics, pulling his arms away from me, reaching for Todd. He eagerly left my bag and went to Sage, checking for any food. He was rewarded eventually when Sage pulled out a small piece of meat for him, Todd snatching it up.

"Do you have a plan?" I asked as he placed Todd on the ground, allowing him to roam around the room.

Sage nodded, placing his suitcase on the floor and sitting on the bed. I joined him, listening as he described his plan in detail. In the end, I realized that what we were doing would either end with us succeeding and freeing the King or failing and finally meeting Death.

Chapter Twenty Eight

Chapter Twenty Eight

"Do you have enough supplies?" I asked, to which she replied with a roll of her eyes.

"Do I need to remind you, the both of you, that this is not my first time journeying outside of the castle? This is my job and I am more than capable of doing it. Focus on your part of the plan. That is where the risks lie, not within my part," Shaterria explained.

She was going off to spread the rumors throughout the closest towns. Rumors were a disease humans continuously fed, most caring none for the person the disease attacked. They would feed it until it burst, twisting and altering into something other than its true form. By then, it had spread, growing larger and larger. Today, we were counting on all of this to happen.

"Good luck," I murmured, Sage remaining silent but tilting his head in her direction. She returned the nod, briefly saying goodbye before she mounted her horse and rode off. All that was left was for Sage and me to do our part.

I had decided that it would be best to leave Todd locked up in a room for a bit. I had chosen the King's room seeing as it was the largest, leaving room for Todd and had sunlight filtering through the windows. However, I knew it wasn't a fit situation for him and could only hope that this would all be over soon so Todd could return to nature.

We were eating in silence, knowing we would need most of our energy. We had fixed toast, eggs, sausage, and biscuits which were all the supplies we'd gotten in our haste. So it seemed that was what we would be eating for the next few days. Or the next few weeks.

Once we finished eating, we cleaned before heading outside and finding the building where all the tools were kept. Together, we grabbed the sacks of screws and nails, hammers, barrels of planks of wood, and many other items making sure to haul as much as we could into the castle. By the time we finished, the tool shed was almost empty.

We thought it would be best to begin with the front of the castle. We boarded up the windows, Sage locking all the rooms with the skeleton key he had. To be sure, we boarded up the rooms as well because it would create enough noise to be heard if someone tried pulling back the wood rather than unlocking a door.

This was our daily routine few several days. We would eat, work, eat, and sleep just to repeat it all over again. We had grown used to it, managing to do so faster and more efficiently as time passed by.

Sage and I talked little while this happened, yet the silence was comfortable. When we did talk, it was about the King or our lives. I learned that Sage had a younger sister he had adored and used to have a lover whom he loved. They had left the castle, as well as leaving Sage. He had contacted them but over the years they had stopped responding. He hoped that when the King's name was cleared, he would be able to contact his sister in hopes of reuniting with her. I silently agreed, hoping that his sister would come visit him.

I told him about my mother, a woman that my father had loved with all his heart. They had cherished one another, even their bickering loving somehow. I told him of how they would walk through the forest together while I tagged along behind with a family dog that had long ago passed away. I told him of the miscarriage my mother had and how after she'd gardened her worries away until she herself wilted and disappeared. I told him that she was part of the forest now, singing with the birds and howling through the wolves. He told me that given that, he could understand why I held so much love for my forest.

When Sage and I finally finished, all the rooms were locked and barricaded, along with all the windows downstairs. We had blocked the halls with objects large enough that they were impossible to subtly get by and you were only able to do so by creating noise. The one doors left alone were my room, which Sage, Todd, and I were sharing at the moment, the castle's entrance, and the hallway to the King's room, and the King's room.

"Do you think it will be enough?" Sage and I were sitting on the floor of our shared room eating dinner. Todd's head was resting on my knee, his eyes flickering quickly between Sage and me, waiting for the moment we looked at him. If we did, his head would raise the slightest in hope. I had shared part of my meat with him and he was convinced one of us would do so again.

"It has to be. There are no other options," Sage grunted, a displeased expression etched onto his face. He was worried that our plan would not work either. I did believe there were flaws, too many almost. However, he was right. There was nothing else we could do short from attempting to bust the King out ourselves.

"And if we succeed?" I looked at him, not understanding his question. His eyes were now on me, studying my reaction. "What will you do if we succeed?" he repeated, clarifying.

I shook my head slightly, wondering what he could possibly think I would do. "What do you mean? I will return home-"

"But you have not finished what you were assigned to do. The King is not tamed." I frowned at his quick response.

"And how are we supposed to know the King is tamed? There are no guidelines to this, Sage. Is he not technically tamed now? He's changed for the better. If you continue going outdoors with him and socializing, all will be fine," I explained but he did not seem to approve yet.

"And if the King turns into a wolf once more? Or what if he loses control?" he questioned and I exhaled sharply.

"I did what I could, Sage. I will stay for a bit longer but I do not feel I can do more. I work with animals. I cannot fix a man's temperament," I said softly and Sage laughed.

"We are running in circles, Rowan. I have explained to you that it is an unyielding woman who craft's a man's heart." I narrowed my eyes, remembering the last time he had spoken those words. We had been much less friendly.

"Perhaps it is not the King that needs an unyielding woman. Perhaps it is you who needs one," I said, laughing. Sage did not notice but his own temperament was in need of fixing as well.

He looked at me, the ghost of a smile playing on his lips. "Are you going to be the woman to do so?" At the simple question, my laughter ceased and color stained my cheeks. He chuckled at my response, saying nothing more as he returned to his food as if nothing had happened.

Before the night ended, Shaterria returned, bringing supplies along with her. We put them away, explaining all we had done and updating her.

"And your journey?" Sage asked her once we finished, leaning against the wall. I stood nearby, both of us looking at her. She smiled briefly, nodding.

"It went well, although it was difficult at first. Many did not want to hear the words of a dead man's messenger. When I was finally able to talk, they listened. I told that the child was still living within the castle walls and would soon rule them. They questioned me of course but I was able to answer as vaguely as possible. Word traveled fast. By the time I visited the last town, old servants were making claimed of hearing cries from the King's room. Some even believed that they had seen the child or heard the King talking to one."

I sighed in relief, satisfied that had gone well. However, the difficult part was yet to be done. We had boarded up the castle and we had spread rumors of the King producing a secret heir to the throne. Yet, now we had to wait.

Chapter Twenty Nine

Chapter Twenty Nine

The day had begun, all of sharing a breakfast meal together before Shaterria left once again. Today, she was to check on any rumors about the King's condition and attempt to make sure all was fine with him for the time being. Soon, we would be of much more help, however, this was all we could do at the moment.

"No."

I frowned, gritting my teeth. Even now, I had forgotten how stubborn he was. His face was a hardened mask without expression. His brown eyes stared into my own, daring me to challenge his reply while his lips were clasped together tightly. Arguing with him never got either one of us anywhere.

"If I go, I am not coming back, Sage," I snapped back, my hands pressed against my hips. "I only need you to check on him. If you leave now, it is not likely that I will be harmed. You do not even have to talk to him. Just make sure he is happy and well," I tried again but Sage simply shook his head.

"Rowan-"

"Sage," I shot back, mimicking his exasperated tone."Please? Todd and I will remain within the castle until you return. I can lock the entrance doors if you prefer as well. You can travel there and back faster than I can. If something does happen, it will likely not be within this morning. So, Shaterria should be back before the sun is gone for the day."

He was quiet for a moment, briefly closing his eyes and pinching the bridge of his nose as if he had a headache. I did not say anything else, allowing him an interval of silence to make his decision. However, if he would not go then I would be the one checking on my father. It had been longer than any of us thought and I was worried.

"You are to lock the entrance as you promised, only unlocking it if I or Shaterria are the ones behind the door. If something happens, you are to hide. Do not try anything on your own, Rowan." His eyes were finally open, his words full of caution while his eyes held a hint of concern.

"I am not as blindly loyal as you, Sage. I am also not dense enough to attempt attacking someone who most likely had the advantage," I replied teasingly, yet Sage did not find the humor in it. I sighed, rephrasing my words. "I will lock the door and keep it locked. Are you satisfied enough to leave now?"

I watched as he relaxed a fraction before nodding. He knelt down, running his hand through Todd's fur while murmuring parting words to him. As he stood up, he looked at me once more. "This is serious. Remain inside until I return," he said, before adding, "I will be back soon with news of your father."

Todd and I walked him outside, watching as Sequeria galloped off, both of them eventually disappearing from our sight. I took Todd inside, closing the door behind the both of us and locking it before turning my attention back to my little one.

"I have not been paying much attention to you have I, my little one?" I asked him, smiling softly when he cocked his head questioningly at me. "I think it is time for a bath. You have not had one in quite some time."

I took Todd with me into the bathroom, hearing his chatter quiet down as the water turned on. Once I turned it back off and put him into the tub, his ears flattened against his skull and his tail lowered. I laughed, watching his ears perked up for a quick moment.

"You act as if I am hurting you, Todd. It will be over in a minute," I said, hoping to reassure him. But he continued to sulk, pleading me to stop my "torturing" all while I merely laughed at him.

"Alright, little one," I said as I finished, draining the water before grabbing a towel. Before I could turn and hold it out to him, he shook himself off. The water droplets flew in every direction, including on me.

Todd started chattering once again as if the bathtime had never happened before he jumped out and flew at me. I laughed, catching him with the towel and wrapping him in it. It was his favorite bit of the whole process, wrestling with the towel.

I sat for a bit, watching and laughing, as Todd darted all around the bathroom, rubbing against me and the other towels I had brought along just for this. However, Todd's frenzied behavior came to a halt as he stood completely still.

"Todd?" I said softly, keeping my voice quiet. His ears were raised, flickering now and again. I could see the fur on his back begin to raise, his tail bristling in seconds. I stiffened, Todd's upper lip curling back as he growled lowly.

"Hush," I whispered, pushing him behind me. He obeyed but remained as alert and nervous as before. I stood, pausing before leaving the room and locking Todd in it. I was sure I had locked the entrance.

I was going against Sage's warning, despite promising him that I would do just the opposite. I searched my room, finding a knife that Sage had supplied me with when I first returned. He had said that all three of us should have something to defend ourselves with in case we were alone.

I crept slowly out of the room, checking the hall, before stepping out. I stood there, listening to anything that might help. While it remained silent, my eyes flickered as they spotted something. The door that led up the stairs towards the King's room was cracked open.

I hesitated, knowing there was nothing else I could do. There was no way to alert Shaterria or Sage fast enough. If I hid, they would find that there was no child and run off, possibly never returning.

I walked up the stairs, doing so quietly. The door leading to the hall was open as well, beckoning me forward. I listened, my steps growing lighter as I continued before taking a deep breath and opening the door.

Chapter Thirty

Chapter Thirty

I do not know what I was expecting. Perhaps a hunter who wanted to boast about killing the legendary King. Maybe in the depths of my mind, I believed that it was a servant or guard who felt as if they had been done wrong and wanted to personally punish the King for their loss. However, standing by the window was none of these.

She appeared to be older, fading into a silver color at its roots while the rest was a darker brown, all of it piled on top of her head. She also wore a large black gown that reminded me of what would be worn to a funeral. The material was thick and rich, something only someone from a background of wealth could afford.

Her head was held high, her arms folded on top of one another in front of her. One of the arms appeared mangled, scars wrapping themselves all around it. Her hand appeared to be missing a finger, the rest drumming along her upper arm.

"Who are you?" I asked, breaking the silence. My voice seemed to create a booming effect, threatening to send a shiver down my spine. I kept still, my eyes never leaving her figure.

She casually turned towards me, a smile appearing on her face. It was a perfect one at that, kind and gentle. Yet, her presence suggested something entirely different. "Forgive me, dear. My name is Anise Sandalius. Formerly known as Queen Sandalius." I blinked, more lost than before.

She had been given the chance to kill the King, long ago when he was given a death sentence for killing her husband. Why had she not accepted if it was her plan now?

"Everything was going according to plan until you came along, Rowan. The King was going to be gone soon enough without my intervening. However, you arrived at the perfect time for him, ruining that. So, I had to come out of hiding and speed up what you were only prolonging."

She finally walked away from the window, coming closer to me with each step she took. Her face did not hold any of the cruelty that her thoughts and words did but perhaps that is why no one ever questioned her. "I am terribly sorry about the fox, dear. However, it seemed I was helping the deformed thing. A creature like that shouldn't be allowed out in the wild. There are dangerous things out in the forest."

I stiffened, refusing to take her bait. Todd had lived in the forest for all his life and not been attacked except for once. He was able to handle himself quite well, however, I was not going to explain that to her.

"Why allow the King to live? You were given the chance to end his life and rejected it," I replied, turning to keep my eyes on her as she began circling me, her back towards the door.

She gave a short laugh, shaking her head as if it was a ridiculous question. "And give him what he wanted? That boy would've gladly welcomed death at the time." Her eyes narrowed, reminding me much of a predatory bird's zeroing in on its prey. "I wanted Kieran to pay for what he did to my husband and me. When his life ended, I wanted him to feel guilt and pain as I am sure he's experienced over these past few months."

I pursed my lips, replying. "Having the King killed will not bring your husband back."

Finally, Anise's facial features twisted into something less kind as she smirked. "No, but it will certainly make me feel much better."

She had been planning this for some time, this much I was sure of. Perhaps she had a backup plan in mind in case things did not go as planned, which is exactly what had happened according to her. If she had not come here, no one would have suspected the widow who had gracefully grieved for her husband and humbly pardoned the King. No one would know of the shadows that lurked behind her or the darkness that had made itself at home within her mind.

"The both of us had given that boy everything he could have ever dreamed of and more!" she snapped, her voice raising abruptly. "We raised him as a proper child yet he fought against us as if we were the indecent ones, not those wolves. And do you know what he did, dear Rowan? He repaid our hospitality and generosity by killing the man that had acted as a father to him and making me flee.

There were no consequences for his actions! So, all I'm doing is returning the favor," she said, getting her emotions under control at the end, composing her expression at the same time.

"You speak nothing but lies. The wolves were his family first and foremost. They were his true caretakers. You and your husband were nothing more than obstacles for him," I spat back, remembering the King's story of how they had treated him.

She once again laughed, this time throwing her head back dramatically. "Family? Those creatures were nothing but killers. They tried killing me when we were hunting them." She raised her disfigured arm, twisting it and turning it to show me the full extent of her injuries.

I scoffed. "No wonder they attempted to kill you. It is only a shame they were not able to finish the job," I said, satisfaction running through me when her eyes flashed with anger.

"Enough talking!" she snapped, growing tired of our charades. "Where is the child?" She no longer appeared to hold the elegance of royalty. Anise now held the composure of a criminal, alert and poised to strike.

"I have nothing else to say to you," I replied, tightening my grip on the knife I held. Her eyes focused on it, flickering before she ran and darted out of the room.

Kieran Sandalius' POV

Every man had a breaking point. It is the point in which everything piling on one's spine grows too heavy, finally snapping it into two. It is the point in which we can no longer deal with the strain that life has placed on us. It is not when we snap that matters but how we deal with the situations at hand.

My breaking point had happened long ago or so I had believed. My life had been altered when I was swept away from the pack of wolves, from my family, and placed into a sheltered building that quickly turned into a prison.

I could remember the very day the witch came to the castle. She had been dressed inconspicuously, going unnoticed by the guards at the time. When she revealed herself, the King and Queen were frightened, calling for someone to whisk her away. I was fascinated.

She had knelt in front of me, promising to make everything better. I had believed her, listening as she told us that she would return me to my parents. It is safe to say that no one expected what happened next.

I was turned into a wolf and when I was human again, the King and Queen locked me in a room. I remained there for some time until they brought an adviser. The adviser told them it was best to treat me as a wolf rather than a human when dealing with me. This way, they would be prepared for the worst before it happened.

They allowed me out of the room but with this came stricter rules. I was not allowed in public alone and curfews became tighter. I was punished more severely for behavior that was considered unnatural by the King and Queen.

I would find myself shifting over the slightest emotion imbalance that occurred. Those days, I was more often a wolf than a human. This continued until one night when the King reached his own breaking point.

He had snapped, yelling that he was done training me. He told his wife that I would never make a good ruler and they should have killed me along with the wolves. She had attempted to reassure him, telling him they would send me away to someone who would be able to straighten out my abnormal behavior. He told her that if she did not find someone within the next few days, he would have me banished from the lands before he punished me yet again.

I suppose I too had reached my breaking point, tired from the harsh treatment I received from the two who called themselves my parents. That night, I shifted and killed the King.

I was sent away and told that I would be killed. I did not put up a fight, pleading them to do so. It was not killing the King that scared me. It was not being able to control my own body, not being able to know what I would do. What would happen if I began to care for another? Would I hurt them as well? To this, I was not willing to wait and find out the answer.

Before they could kill me, however, the Queen put a stop to it all. She pardoned me, leaving the castle and all its land to me. I returned, growing worse than before. I learned it was easiest to control myself when others were not alone so I began to avoid people, only doing what was needed. I locked myself in a single room, leaving Sage to deal with anything in the castle and Shaterria anything outside of its walls.

Now, I was in yet another prison, this one much more real. This time they had placed shackles around my ankles, wrists, and neck. The chains led to the wall, bolted into the stone. The room itself was a small one lacking room to walk in. However, given my current situation, I was not able to walk as is.

Most of the days were spent drifting in and out of sleep. The first few, they had attempted to break me, whipping my bare back. That was ended when I shifted, the shackles on my ankles and wrist no longer fitting causing me to hang myself as a wolf. So I was left alone, someone only coming by to present me with food and take out the bucket of waste.

I had gathered that by tomorrow, I could be killed. It would be done publicly because so many had argued that they had been harmed by me and it was only fair that they were able to watch as I took my last breath.

Soon enough, I would be free of this world and able to run with the wolves once again.

9 781805 107330